A Billionaire's Game

Erica Frost

Published by Erica Frost, 2023.

This is a work of fiction. Similarities to real people, places, or events are entirely coincidental.

A BILLIONAIRE'S GAME

First edition. January 5, 2023.

ISBN: 979-8223436362

Written by Erica Frost.

Table of Contents

A Billionaire's Game
Opposites Attract Office Romance

By: Erica Frost

Foreword

A billionaire is never easily ensnared…

A new job means a new beginning. A new possibility. But also, a new love affair.

The moment I saw him, I knew he could not be more wrong for me. Sizzling hot. Unapproachable. Hard-working. My boss. Rocco Barbati. The Italian in his name as lascivious as his smile.

I don't even try to keep away. I can't. He draws me in like a magnet. Our opposites are too attracted to resist. Salacious and sensual, he awakens something in me. But with him, it's two steps forward, one step back. One hand pulls me in, while the other keeps me at bay. His switches between hot and cold are too much to take.

So, I need to step up my game and show him two can play it better than one.

A Billionaire's Game

A Billionaire's Game

Chapter 1

Grace

"If this isn't the best reason to celebrate, then I don't know what is!"

Alisa's resounding declaration assures me there is no room for any back-talk. I guess, she is right. We really do have a good reason. Plus, Alisa is a champ at finding perfectly plausible excuses to celebrate, which makes her an excellent choice of not only a roommate, but also a best friend.

"Isn't it a general rule to get a good night's rest before the first day at your new job," I chuckle, seated comfortably on the sofa to our two-bedroom apartment.

"Oh, pish, posh," she waves her hand at me dismissively, crossing her left leg over the other, flashing me a broad smile. "You need to walk in there with confidence, girl, and what better way to gain confidence than chatting with some cuties over a glass of wine."

Confidence has never been Alisa's issue. Built like a model, with long fiery red hair and eyes the color of summer grass, she's always been the epitome of a goddess. Flawlessly gorgeous. I guess, that's why she spent most of her late teens posing for famous photographers. Then, according to her, she just got bored with it at some point, and now, she finished school and works as a vet assistant. Long way from a model just standing there, looking pretty.

"So?" Her question brings me back to reality. "We'll be there just in time for happy hour, have a drink and come back home by nine. The latest."

"You mean, I'll come back home. You might not, you fox," I chuckle.

"Well, it's not easy being pretty, I bear the burden," she laughs. Looking so effortlessly beautiful might be something someone could resent her, but it's impossible to feel that way about her.

"It's lucky the animals there don't really understand what you're saying," I tease. "Or, they'd feel about you like the rest of us."

We chuckle some more, then I realize it's well past noon. My plan is to walk past the building where I'm supposed to start work tomorrow. The idea already gives me strange, but pleasant goosebumps.

"You're lucky you're so starry-eyed right now and I just don't have the heart to tease you back," she nods.

"I am?" I wonder.

Then, I realize I already know the answer to that. This new job already feels like a brand-new love affair, something I've been searching for all my life. I always wanted to make my own way to the top, to get a job based on my own skills and expertise, as opposed to pulling a few connections, which my cop dad was more than able, and I guess also happy to do. ButI was strict in my refusal.

Instead, this new job opened up. I applied. And, the rest was fate. Although only an entry-level position, I feel ecstatic about starting off as an assistant to Tim Hoffman over at Visionetworks, that are considered to be one of the leading advertising agencies not only in the city but in all of US.

"Well, I'll leave that starry-eyed look for tomorrow then," I continue, getting up. "I want to head across town to do some errands. Maybe even get some new work clothes. I need to look as professional as possible, and you know that's not my to go look."

"I know," she nods. "Chuck Taylor will feel forever betrayed."

"Oh, ha, ha," I pretend to laugh, throwing a nearby pillow at her, which she catches easily.

"Maybe you'll finally get rid of those darn sneakers."

"You can keep hoping," I chuckle.

"We on for that drink then?" she wonders. "Don't stand me up now."

"Fine," I nod. "But I need to be back by nine, I'm serious."

"So am I," she assures me, her green eyes flaring up at me.

"Then, OK. I'll be back in time to get ready."

Within the next hour, I'm out of the house, and I'm immediately overwhelmed by the sensations of life that passes by me. I've been living in this city my entire life, and yet, it seems that, in every new stage of life, some new, still unknown part of it is beckoning me to explore it. This is exactly the feeling I have right now.

The doorman nods at me, with a smile.

"Lovely day, Miss Hensley," he tells me.

He is about the age of my father, and with that same endearing smile about him that makes you want to talk to him every time you see him. Some people are just like that. Magnets for other people. While some people are magnets turned the other way around, pushing you away.

"It really is, Mr. Davidson," I nod at him. "I'll enjoy it while I still can, before it gets dreadfully hot in July."

He nods at me again, and we part ways amicably, as always. I walk over to my car, and the moment I join the rest of the traffic, I can feel everything around me. The hot air. The exhaust pipes churning angrily. The street vendors. Life keeps going. It doesn't matter if you choose to halt yourself or not. It will simply pass you by.

I spend the following two hours shopping for new clothes and end up with a disappointing amount of only one shite shirt and a simple royal blue pencil skirt. For now, that'll have to do.

I check my watch, and I realize that I still have enough time before heading back to the apartment to get ready for our celebratory drink. Suddenly, an idea pops to mind. I could drop by the building I am to start tomorrow, and just check the place out. Without much need to be convinced of this, I head there, making sure to park somewhere close. I was given a card that would probably allow me a special parking spot inside ethe building itself, but I didn't want to do that right now. I merely wanted to enter the building, take a look around, buzz myself up the elevator, then down, then head back home. Just something to pass the time.

I feel something beckoning me to go in. I tap my blazer pocket, just to make sure I brought my newly issued ID. Then, I head boldly towards the building which seemed to tear the skies in two. An onslaught of people rushes at me almost at the same time, and I feel like I have to elbow my way through. Alisa would say it's kind of symbolic. After all, I fought all those people interviewing for the same job and I won. I sure did.

Upon entering the building, the pristine whiteness of the walls around me hits me like the sun at the top of a mountain. For a moment, I feel like I need my sunglasses, but a moment later, my eyes adjust. The two guards dressed immaculately in black business suits give me a weird look. It's my clothes. The official clothes I'm supposed to be wearing tomorrow are still in my car, in the new bag.

I whip out my ID. One of them frowns, but then nods. I have been granted passage into this marvelous place of dark framed revolving doors and marble floors stricken with silver veins. All around me, I can see polished aluminum, glistening.

I head straight for the elevators, pressing the button with my index finger. My red nail blossoms before me, and now I'm glad Alisa convinced me to get my nails done a few days ago. The door opens with a loud ping, and two women walk out of it, talking in a hushed manner. I go in, watching as the door closes. I press for the fifteenth floor.

I notice that the elevator has a glass floor only when it starts moving. And, I immediately start to breathe more heavily. Generally, I'm not a fan of heights. Especially when I can see my separation from the ground floor becoming larger and larger.

My heart starts pounding loudly. I can almost hear it drumming inside my ears. I watch as the numbers light up, counting to the one that would allow me to run out of this glass box.

Ten. Eleven. Thirteen. Just a little more. Fourteen. Fifteen.

Finally, the elevator stops. It takes two more seconds to open the door, and I'm already leaning against the wall with my left hand. I need to get out. I already see little stars at the corner of my eyes. Shit. I guess I'll have to try doing this with my eyes closed or something.

The moment the doors slide open, not even fully so, I run outside as if my life depends on it. But I realize too late that because of my rushing, someone didn't have enough time to move to the side, and I end up bumping straight at a man who was standing there.

What makes it even worse, he was holding a cup of coffee, which now lay as a soaked-up smudge on his obviously custom-made three-piece suit. My eyes widen with shock, as I lift my gaze to meet his. If I should describe his body as a perfect specimen of magnificent maleness, then I should definitely describe his face as the most handsome face I've ever seen.

"I..." I say, still in shock, but now I have no idea what to focus on first. The fact that he is Adonis in the flesh, or that I made this perfect man spill his coffee and I probably ruined his suit. "I'm so sorry..." I manage to gasp.

At that moment, he stares back at me, and I can see a shield sliding down, revealing the piercingly striking blue of his eyes. I feel even dizzier than back inside the elevator, and I'm thinking, that was exactly where I should have stayed.

"I... I'll pay for dry-cleaning," I say, realizing that I'm just digging myself even deeper here. I should just keep quiet, but his savage gorgeousness is making me even more nervous.

He looks down at his body, impressing a sense of unrelenting power upon me. He assesses the damage, and while his head is bent downward, I can see the sharp outlines of his jaw, his strikingly Roman nose and firmly etched mouth, that lay slightly parted at this moment.

I take a step back, feeling overpowered by his manhood, by his cologne, which seems to have entered my every pore. Without a word, he hands me the now empty coffee cup, revealing his bright silver cuff links in the shape of a lion's head and a watch which probably costs more than what I make in half a year.

I take the cup in my hands. Only then do I realize that I have a handkerchief in my pocket. I quickly take it out, and without even thinking, I press it onto his chest. He doesn't move, only lifts his eyebrow in surprise.

Fingers feel the hard core of his body immediately. A body that probably works out more than just the advised two hours every week. Even through the damp fabric of his clothes, our touch electrifies me. His brows arrogantly slash at me, and I immediately pull back.

"That won't help much," he tells me in a sharply intelligent voice.

"I'm sorry," I repeat again. "I... the floor... I got dizzy and..."

"The floor?" he wonders, maintaining eye contact at all times, his voice all smooth like honey. That's actually what makes this conversation so difficult.

"Glass floor inside the elevator," I finally manage to explain. "I got dizzy and rushed outside.

"Oh," he nods.

I realize that he's younger than I first thought. Now, I see that he's in his thirties, but those eyes seem ancient. Worldly. Experienced. He's drawing me in, as if there's a rope around my waist and he just needs to reel me in, like a caught fish.

"Maybe not a good idea to work in a building where all the elevators have glass floors," he suggested. "You look a little flushed. Maybe try sitting down for a minute."

I know I'm flushed. But that has little to do with that dizziness. It's him, and I doubt he doesn't know that, looking all civilized and outrageously gorgeous, but I see that raw animal clawing to be released from underneath that suit. His eyes aren't letting me go, and it makes my brain shift into the wrong gear.

"I'm fine," I nod, trying to regain my senses, and convince myself he's just a good-looking guy. Nothing else. Thousands of those walking in the streets.

Only, that's not really true. This man is unlike any other I've ever seen before. And, I'm not really off to a very good start, as I occasionally glance at the smudge on his suit. I want to run away, because I know I can't handle the heat of his gaze much longer.

Get a grip, Grace. You've made a fool of yourself once. Just accept it and move along.

Suddenly, his eyebrow raises, and he looks like he wants to say something else. If there is anything else to say, that is. He glances behind me. Then, he extends his hand. It passes right by my ear, leading to his entire body moving forward. Closer to mine.

The smell of his cologne washes over me, invading my nostrils. My lips tense, pressing tightly against each other. I hear the soft pressing of the elevator button behind me. Just as quickly as he leaned over, he pulls away, leaving me with an intoxicating mixture of his cologne and the warmth of his breath which grazed my cheek.

The elevator door opens, and he raises his eyebrow at me.

"Oh," I realize clumsily what he's referring to.

I'm in the way, so I move. He seems to chuckle silently to himself, then walks into the elevator. I don't turn around. I'm guessing he doesn't either. I listen to the sound of the door closing, and then, I sigh with relief.

Great. Just great.

Chapter 2

Grace

When I enter the big, glass revolving door of the Visionetworks building that morning, the memory of the previous day's mishap is still fresh in my mind. Of course, I had to share it with Alisa during our quick visit to the nearest bar the previous evening, and she assured me that I was blowing it out of proportion, something, I admit, I'm prone to do often.

So, on the way here, I kept reminding myself that what happened the previous day was just an accident. Nothing that would change my first day or in any way haunt me. I mean, why would it? That guy probably doesn't even work here. He was dressed too nicely. Maybe he was one of those high-class clients. In any case, I can only hope that our paths won't cross again. Even though I know I'll never be able to forget the look of those deep cerulean eyes.

As I stand in front of the elevator, I'm trying to come to terms with myself. I want to make the best first impression, so I opted for a nice, forest green curve hugging dress, with my black Oxford shoes, which were polished to perfection this morning. I decided against heels, just in case I need to rush here and there. I need to see how much walking I'll be doing on a daily basis, and then make the right choice on my shoes.

My dark, chestnut hair is pulled back in a sleek ponytail. Simple and chic, at the same time. A pair of small dainty earrings adorn my ears, a present from my parents. I realize I've forgotten my watch. Not that I'd be looking at it often, but I like to know where I stand timewise. Especially on my first day.

"New?"

I suddenly hear a voice behind me. I turn around, and I realize it belongs to a young woman about my age, only she seems much more confident, like she knows exactly where she's going and how to get there. Me? I'm still considering how to sort out the glass floor issue and get to the fifteenth floor.

"That obvious, huh?" I chuckle a little nervously, but her smile assures me that she understands. After all, she herself must have been new here, too.

"You've got that look," she clarifies, pressing the button of the elevator.

My heart immediately starts beating faster. I'm still not sure I'll be walking that distance up or take the elevator.

"Do you know where you're going?" she asks politely, revealing a row of pearly white teeth, framed with red lipstick, which perfectly matches her cherry dotted blouse and black pencil skirt. In her hand, she is holding a briefcase, as one single diamond ring flashes on her hand.

"Fifteen," I tell her, as the door pings open before us.

She steps in first, but I don't move. She holds the door, immediately recognizing what's behind my hesitation.

"It's the floor, isn't it?" she smiles, her eyes dark green and warm.

"Let's just say I've already had one unpleasant meeting with this floor," I explain, frowning. "I'm on the verge of just taking the stairs and risk reaching my post a sweaty mess."

"On your first day? I wouldn't risk it," she advises me gently. "Come."

Then, she extends her hand towards me. Obviously, she expects me to take it. I'm still a bit uncertain, but she's been so nice, and I can't refuse her help. So, I take her by the hand, and slowly, one foot at a time, I enter the elevator.

"Just don't look down, OK?" she tells me. "Just look at me."

Which, in all honesty, isn't all that hard to do. She is a stunning woman, with sharp dark hair styled in a modern pixie cut, which compliments her face wonderfully.

"I'm Sonya," she introduces herself, with my hand still in hers.

"Grace," I nod, trying not to look down, and instead focus on her face, on her eyes. It's difficult, because I can feel us moving, and I don't even need to look down to know that the ground is disappearing from sight.

"Nice to meet you, Grace," she replies. "Just breathe. Slowly. Do it with me."

Somehow, I don't feel silly at all, doing breathing exercises in an elevator with a total stranger. I take a deep breath, keeping it in for a few moments, then I exhale.

"Good," she nods. "Now, try again."

So, I repeat the whole process again, and at this point, the drumming in my ears has subsided a little. Then, the elevator releases that liberating noise and the door opens. Sonya walks out with me.

"I... I don't know how to thank you for what you did," I gush, still in disbelief that even the cut-throat corporate world boasts a few kind people.

"It's fine," she says. "I like to think that good deeds are like a never-ending chain of good events. Just do something nice for someone else, and keep the chain going."

"That's a wonderful thought," I reply, amazed by this beautiful, wonderful woman who has made the beginning of this day into something magical.

"Well, I should be off, I'm up on the twenty-second," she tells me. "Maybe I'll see you around, Grace. And, just remember, focus on something and breathe. It's just an elevator, nothing else."

"I guess you're right," I sigh, knowing that it sounds much easier in theory than in practice.

She waves, then a moment later, the elevator door closes behind her, and I'm left to continue on the path of my first day alone. Only now, I'm filled with a sense of awe, and anticipation. If something so nice could happen first thing on my arrival here, I wonder what else could happen.

I walk over to the crescent-shaped desk, and the lady seated there. She's got a Bluetooth earphone in her left ear, and she lifts her right index finger, gesturing at me to wait a moment.

"Yes, I'll let him know, thank you," she finishes quickly, then her attention is back on me.

I show her my ID, with a slightly awkward smile.

"Oh, Miss. Hunter, "she reads my name, and a flash of recognition appears in those brown eyes. "It's your first day, isn't it? I hope it goes wonderfully."

"Grace, please," I correct her. "And, is everyone around here this nice?"

"Well, we do try," she chuckles. "Take some time to settle in, Mr. Hoffman will be with you shortly. Do you need me to take you to your desk?"

"Oh, no, thank you," I shake my head. "I'm sure I can find my way around here easily. If not, it's a good orientation exercise."

She chuckles at my words, and I only then remember her name. Amanda.

"Do let me know if you need anything," she says welcomingly, then the phone rings, and her attention is once more back where it belongs during office hours.

I wave at her, doubtful she's seen me, and I walk down an elongated hallway, enjoying the view that spread out the windows. I can enjoy the view around me. Just not the one below me. I guess I've always been one of those people who liked to stand firmly, with both feet on the ground.

I reach the end of the hallway and take a right turn. I immediately find my cubicle, tucked in neatly right by a glass door with the name Tim Hoffman on it. The blinds are drawn, only the door allows a quick peek inside. But I resist the urge. I should be in that office pretty soon. Why rush things?

I take a deep breath, absorbing my new work area. The desk is ivory colored, smooth. The computer in front of me is switched off. I put my purse on the chair. I brought a few things with me, to make this place a little less generic and a little more mine. So, I extract a photo of my family from a few years back, when we visited Niagara Falls. I've also brought my own fountain pen. I'm a bit of a stickler when it comes to using my own writing utensils, and it's something Alisa always makes fun of. Being my best friend, she is allowed to.

My own notebook, too. A glass figurine of a cat, something familiar to hang in there, kitty. Only the glass version.

The place still looks empty. Devoid of my presence there, but I'm guessing it's one of those things that changes with the passage of time. The more time you spend here, the more of a footprint you leave. As always.

I'm surprised to see that most of the other cubicles are empty. At that moment, I hear the sound of oncoming footsteps.

"Grace, good morning."

I turn around immediately and meet a pair of dark eyes underneath a set of bushy eyebrows.

"I see you're starting to settle in," he continues.

"Good morning, Mr. Hoffman, and yes, little by little," I reply, still a little nervous, almost feeling as if this is a dream I'll wake up from any moment. And yet, the dream keeps going.

Mr. Hoffman is about the age of my dad, but his facial hair is still strikingly dark. His glasses sit on the upper bridge of his nose, and they occasionally slide downward, forcing him to use his thick index finger to push them back. He is dressed in a casual suit, no tie.

"Why don't you join me in my office?" he suggests.

"Of course," I immediately nod.

I follow him to his office, and once inside, he gestures at the chair opposite his at his desk, which is a strange combination of dark wood and silver chrome. Perhaps it's one of those acquired tastes. The more you look at it, the more you like it.

I sit down, and he walks around the desk, settling into his chair. To his right, there is a large window, offering a breathtaking view of skyscrapers and clear blue sky. The office isn't big, but it's worth it just for the view.

"Nervous?" he wonders, as he slides a few stray papers to the side, next to his open, but switched off Mac.

"A little," I admit. No point in lying when you could see it from a mile away.

"Not to worry," he assures me, with a confident poise which comforts me.

A boss who knows what he wants and how he wants it done is a good boss. A boss who has no idea what he's doing or how he wants it done always tends to blame others for his mistakes. Luckily, he seems to belong to the former group.

"I'm not a demanding boss," he continues. "Just ask my previous assistant."

My curiosity instantly prods me to try and find out what happened to him or her. I mean, if the position were so good, why would anyone leave on their own?

"She worked for me for over ten years," he explains, as if he somehow read my mind. "Then, she got married, and because her new husband plays pro baseball, they moved out of state."

"I see," I nod, relieved that he actually might be a good boss in that case.

"I guess what I'm trying to say is that I have a certain way of doing things, and once you're acquainted with it, you shouldn't have any problems."

"I'm sure that will be so," I nod. After all, how hard is it to follow instructions and orders?

"Now, do you drink coffee?"

"It's one of my favorite things in the world," I chuckle both at his question and at my answer.

"That makes two of us then," he smiles back. "How about we go over to the break room, and I show you how the new coffee machine works? To be honest, it looks like a miniature space rocket, and I'm still not sure why it won't make a double espresso when I press that button. Maybe we can figure it out together."

"That sounds just fine," I grin, welcoming the thought of a coffee, although I already had one.

"Then, once we figure that out, I could show you some of the accounts I'm working on, and Tina's notes should be somewhere in here. I just need to find them."

I figured Tina is the ex-assistant who went on to live another kind of life, leaving room for me in this one. Thanks, Tina.

Mr. Hoffman stands up first, and I immediately follow suit.

"Now, let's see about that coffee," he tells me, heading out.

I take a deep breath, feeling still a little nervous, but happy that I finally got the ball rolling. From the looks of it, there's nothing but clear skies straight ahead.

That is, at least, what I thought.

Chapter 3

Grace

The day passes by relatively peacefully. Mr. Hoffman and I have been inseparable for the last several hours, and even though I know it's not his job to babysit me throughout the process of my introduction, I appreciate that he does.

He is the epitome of patience, as he walks me through the accounts he's been working on. Then, we both endure a long meeting with the creative team. Not that the guys are annoying or incompetent, it's just that when you're stuck on a problem, sometimes, it's hard to find a way to solve it, or even go around it. Seeing Mr. Hoffman still patient, even in the face of problems, makes me more than just hopeful about the prospects of staying in this company for a long time.

It's about ten to six when we both find each other in his office again. He's had his last coffee for the day, fifth if I remember correctly. He's seated in his chair, just like in the morning, and I have that pleasant rounded, full circle feeling of a job well done, on my first day, nonetheless.

"Well, I guess that should be that for the day," he says with a shrug. "Unless, you have any questions?"

"I have a lot," I smile. "But, honestly, I wouldn't know where to start asking them."

He chuckles at my words. "I know the feeling. I was a newbie once. A long time ago, but it's a feeling you never forget. And, it's the same for everyone."

I nod in agreement.

"Maybe we should just leave any questions you have for tomorrow," he suggests. "You know, let today settle in. Then, we continue tomorrow."

"Sure," I smile.

"We should go over- "

A sudden ringing of his phone interrupts him, and he reaches into his pocket.

"Yes?" he answers. "Mr. Barbati, hello... yes... yes, I have. Should I send it over?... OK... OK... sure thing. I'll send my assistant up immediately with the documents."

He hangs up the phone, then looks around the desk.

"I had a contract somewhere around here," he says, although he's not really paying attention to me. He's obviously looking for something which he can't seem to find.

"We were filing some stuff earlier this afternoon," I suggest. "Is it possible that it's among those papers?"

"Could be," he nods, getting up and walking over to the shelf in the corner.

His finger trails the line of hard covers, then finally he extracts one. "Let's see..."

He puts all the papers inside of it on the table, checking each single one. Quickly, he finds what he's looking for.

"There we go," he smiles. "I doubt I'd remember filing it here. It's not supposed to be here."

"I'm sorry," I immediately apologize.

It's possible that I put it there. But it's also possible that I was just following instructions. In either case, something's urging me to apologize whether or not it's really my fault. His smile assures me we're good.

"It's fine," he nods. "Before you head out, could I ask you to take this up to Mr. Barbati's office, on the twenty-second floor?"

I swallow heavily at the idea. The twenty-second floor was no walking distance. I'd have to take the elevator to go there.

"Grace, are you alright?" His voice brings me back to reality. "You suddenly got a little pale."

Should I tell him? Probably not. I've just started working in an office on the fifteenth floor. Of course, it's expected of me to use the elevator on a regular basis, and if that poses an issue for me, I'm sure they'd easily find someone to replace me. I can't let that happen.

"Yes," I nod, with as much confidence as I can muster. "Everything is fine. I'll be happy to take this upstairs, to Mr. ..." I pause on purpose, offering him a chance to remind me of the name.

"Barbati," he fills me in immediately. "Rocco Barbati. He's my boss' boss."

"Oh," I pretend to be all shocked, but he realizes it's a joke. "I'm to meet the boss of all bosses on my first day? That doesn't seem fair."

He laughs. "Honestly, I'd take it up to him myself, but I promised my wife I'd be home by seven. It's our youngest daughter's birthday, you see."

"Of course!" I nod enthusiastically, completely forgetting all about my crippling fear of heights. "You should head on home immediately, if you want to beat the traffic."

"Thanks for that," his voice is kind, and I know he appreciates the help on this one. "If I take it up to him, I'm afraid I might stay longer than intended, and I assure you, if I miss my girl's birthday, my wife will make me sleep out in the yard with the dog."

I chuckle. "That also doesn't seem fair."

"Not at all," he shrugs, sighing and getting up at the same time. "But that's corporate life for ye. Plus, I doubt Mr. Barbati would have any understanding for family issues."

"No?"

"You know what they say, if you want to be the best in something, it comes at a great cost," he explains. "And, Mr. Barbati hasn't built his empire overnight. It took many nights, I'm sure."

Many nights of what? I guess, Mr. Hoffman is referring to sleepless nights. But sleepless nights can have many causes. Still, I choose not to deepen this conversation. I'll bear the horrible experience of taking the elevator up to the twenty-second, and then I'll just go back down. No more stops in the middle, on the fifteenth.

"Here's the document," he slides it over to me across the polished surface of his desk. "I owe you one for this."

"Don't worry about it, Mr. Hoffman," I smile. "I hope your little girl has a lovely birthday."

"Thank you, Grace," he smiles back. "And don't worry. You're doing just fine."

He rushes out upon those words, and I follow immediately after, realizing that everyone else has already left. The entire fifteenth floor is empty. I hoped I'd get the chance to get a better feel of the whole layout of the offices and where what is, but I won't be stopping here on the way down from the twenty-second floor.

The very thought sends shivers down my spine. I have to step into that glass coffin again. I grab the document, then my bag. I glance around. It's calm and empty. I shut down my laptop, waiting until the screen turned dark. Then, I walk over to the elevators.

A cold claw of unease taps me on the shoulders. Hello, again. I have no idea how I'm going to keep doing this day in, day out. Strangely, I have no problem with elevators that have regular floors. Only these glass ones. And whose stupid idea was that anyway?

I welcome the onset of anger. That's always a better option than being scared. Anger gives you courage which you usually wouldn't have. This time, that is the courage to step into the elevator.

A ding alerts me to the arrival of my nightmare. The door opens, like a pair of arms, warm and welcome. I hesitate for just a moment.

Don't be ridiculous. Hundreds of people take it every day, in this very building. So, can you.

I take a deep, painful sigh. Then, my foot starts on its own. It's better just to let the physical part of my brain take over. But, the moment the door closes, I feel a slight shiver take over me. My finger lifts to the buttons, pressing the right one.

The elevator moves noiselessly. I just have to make sure not to look down. So, I don't. I start humming the last song I heard on the radio. I even manage to lip sync. All just so I wouldn't look down.

A few moments later, I start getting dizzy. But, luckily, I follow the numbers lighting up. Just two more.

Three seconds later, and the door opens once more. I barge out of the elevator, swallowing suspicious amounts of saliva, that probably would have provoked something nastier. But I survived. And, honestly, it was one millionth part less scary than this morning. If I ride it a million times more, hopefully, I should be fine at some point.

I release a sigh of relief. I look down the elongated hallway. It looks almost deserted. I start walking, and huge windows expose the entire city before me. I swallow heavily again, feeling that dizziness dangerously close by. So, I move all the way to the other side of the wall.

I focus on the only door at the end of the hallway. It's a double door, with a golden tag on the right side. I'm still too far away to see what it says. I get closer slowly, realizing that not many people get to walk down this hallway.

For some reason, I'm nervous. I know that's silly, and completely unreasonable, but I can't help it. I smooth out an invisible wrinkle on my skirt, then I lift my hand and knock on the door.

At first, there is no reply. I frown. Why would you call for someone to drop off the papers, if you decide to leave before that?

Still, I wait a moment longer, and it is then that I hear a voice from within.

"Yes?"

I press on the golden, lion's mouth doorknob, and open the door. I glance over at the huge, dark oak desk at the other end of the room. A man sitting at it lifts his gaze, and his green eyes meet mine. My breath stops.

It is the man with the coffee.

Chapter 4

Grace

It's him. No question about it. I would never forget those eyes. That look that shot me straight in the heart. And somewhere else, but that's not to be mentioned out loud. This time, the effect he has on me is the same.

He lowers his head, but before he does it, he gestures at me quickly with his hand to come over. Then, he continues to look at the laptop before him.

Not knowing what else to do, I tiptoe over to his desk, stopping at what seems to be a safe distance from him. Even though his head is bent down, I see his silver tie, which blends in perfectly with his brilliantly white shirt. His hair is thick, dark, and shiny. Roguishly so.

I have no idea how long I'm standing there, but I do so, nonetheless. I'm barely breathing. The lack of any noise is so complete, that I'm afraid I would somehow taint the sanctity of it by releasing any kind of a sound. My hands are clenching against the document I hold.

Finally, he lifts his head again. His gaze is puzzled. Is it possible that he doesn't know why I'm here?

"Mr. Hoffman sent me up," I explain.

"You brought what I requested?" he asks in an authoritative voice, smoky and dark.

"Yes," I nod quickly, taking another step towards his desk, and putting the document on it. "Here."

He takes it but doesn't thank me for it. Instead, his eyes skim through the paper. He's not looking at me, so it's safe to inspect him more closely. He's even more handsome than I remembered. Strikingly so. The way it gets into you, through your skin and all your defenses, and settles into your very bones, so you can never ever escape that knowledge again, and you continue to compare every other man with him.

He is handsome in away that carries no gentleness. The depth of his eyes is not safe. Those are murky waters you know will strip you bare, but you still want to do it. You want to drown in them. You want to be the one he will remember all of his life, because that is exactly what he becomes for you the moment you see him.

I wonder if he recognized me as the one who probably ruined his shirt. I doubt it. He hasn't looked at me long enough to actually notice me. A part of me wishes he would just continue staring at the document in his hands, while a different part of me, the bold part of me, wants him to look up and see me. To actually see me and recognize me.

As if he's able to hear my thoughts, he lifts his gaze. Awareness strikes right through me, prickling my skin. He doesn't say anything. My heart is racing, my lips parted. I'm on the verge of teasing him, asking him about his shirt, but I don't. I don't want to gamble my luck on my first day. Everything has been going swimmingly, until now. I want to keep it that way for the next ten minutes, until I exit the building.

"This is all?" he suddenly asks.

"Uhm… all?" I repeat, confused.

"Hoffman didn't give you anything else?" No trite politeness with him.

"Well, no, not really," I shake my head. "Was he supposed to?"

He lowers his gaze again. He lifts the single paper in his hand, turns it around. He doesn't seem satisfied. He is showing me his wolf-self, the one that has just gotten back from the depths of the woods. Now, he seems to belong here, but not fully. There is something about him that will never be fully sated, never be completely home in one place.

"It has only one signature," he says.

I'm not really sure what that means. Is it supposed to have more? And, whose signature? So many questions, but I don't ask any of them. I bear his look, just waiting to be dismissed.

"Did Hoffman discuss the Collins account with you?"

"Yes," I immediately nod, even though his question once again catches me off guard.

His gaze is so intense, I feel it burning a hole right through my flesh. Completely focused on me, I know I can't bear it much longer. His left arm is now resting on the desk before him, the tip of his index finger gently tapping against the shiny surface. I barely hear the sound, but I see the motion, and that is enough.

He is demanding, drawing you in without any contact. That is exactly where the allure lies. He seems desireless. Everything he states is a fact. An obligation. His motives are clear. As I stand closer, I see the beginnings of crow's feet in the corner of his eyes. They look so good on him.

"He discussed the concept with you?" he asks again.

"Um, yes," I confirm, feeling a little more at ease now that we're discussing work. That is, after all, why I'm here, and that is all I want to discuss with him, despite that aching yearning deep inside my stomach, which threatens to go lower, if I continue to think about him. So, I don't. I stop... if I can.

"What's your opinion?"

I try to focus on the mechanics of the questions he's asking me. That should be easier than thinking how good he would look on the beach.

"I think it'll work," I shrug stupidly, angry with myself that I couldn't come with anything more solid that that.

He's still impassive. "How?"

"Well..." I know I have only one single second to come up with the right response. I didn't think I'd have to explain my boss to his boss' boss, but obviously, this first day of work was unlike any other. "The budget is set, but the largest demographic will be drawn to its appeal-"

"Why?" he interrupts me.

"Well, there are certain appealing aspects to the concept, which make it sound luxurious while still on a budget. I could see soccer moms going for it as much as CEO's."

"I see," he nods, finally lowering his gaze again.

I can't say if he's happy with my reply or not. There is not a single instance of emotion on his face which might reveal how he feels about any of my replies. Then again, he doesn't look like the type of man who wouldn't say when he doesn't like something. I guess he'd be very vocal about it.

"CEO's?" he frowns. Obviously, he didn't like it.

Honestly, it just popped to me, like a good extreme between two categories of people. Right now, I just want to be parachuted out of this place.

"Do you know any CEO's?" he asks again.

"Um, no, not really," I shake my head, not really sure what it is I said so wrong.

"If you did, you'd know they weren't our target group here."

"I know, I just meant- "

"Maybe you meant, but you didn't think before that."

I frown. He obviously needs to learn more about positive criticism, because he knows jack about it.

"Still, that was a good observation."

My frown is immediately cleared up. But I don't smile. I remain professional. For a moment, he reminds me of a mafia boss. The Italian in him is good enough for it, but it's not only that. It's the way he carries himself.

"That would be all, Miss...?" he ends his statement in a manner of a question.

"Hensley," I introduce myself. "Grace Hensley."

His eyebrow furrows. "You're Hoffman's new assistant?"

"Yes," I confirm.

His lips part, as if he's trying to say something else, but he immediately closes them, nodding more to himself than to me.

"Good," he says impassively.

He turns his attention towards his laptop, and something tells me that I'm dismissed. I'm not even sure how to react to this. Should I just tiptoe out of the room, silently as a church mouse? Or should I whisper a goodbye and then leave? I opt for the former.

Slowly, barely making any sound, I walk out of the room, gently pressing on the doorknob, which eases under the pressure immediately. I walk out, then immediately close the door behind me, leaning onto it, as if in a desire to keep him safely locked up inside.

My heart is still beating like a crazy metronome, keeping absolutely no rhythm. The tempo raises with every thought of the man whose office I just left, and I know it'll take me a while to cool down.

Then I remember that I need to take the elevator down to go home. Crap.

Chapter 5

Grace

"I honestly don't see a reason to go," I sigh, standing in front of the mirror of my bedroom.

Alisa is lying on the bed, her one knee bent, while the other sways carelessly off the edge. On her stomach, there is a bowl of chips, which she's been crunching on for the past fifteen minutes. Usually, it rubs me the wrong way, but this Friday, I'm too distracted to care.

"You're joking, right?"

Crunch. Ugh, that sound.

"No," I frown.

My first week on the job has been easy-going. Occasionally hectic, but that seemed to last only for a brief hour or so, and then Mr. Hoffman and I would be back to the usual grind, which seemed pleasant and not at all stressful.

Then, this morning, he's told me about a company party that's been arranged in the last minute, because someone is retiring, and they wanted to say goodbye properly. Honestly, I don't even know this lady. I feel a little awkward attending the party.

"It's a company event," Alisa explains. "You're part of the company. You get my point?"

Crunch.

"That's some good chips, isn't it?" I chuckle.

"Want some?" she offers the bowl to me, but I shake my head.

I'm looking at my reflection in the mirror. I'm wearing a yellow dress, which hugs my curves down to the waist, then falls freely right underneath by my knees. It's nothing fancy, but it makes me feel good in all the right ways, and I guess it shows.

"I'd rather just stay home," I sigh. "It's been a long week, and I'd welcome some down time with just you- "

"We'll have enough time for us girls tomorrow," she corrects me. "I'll take you to your favorite café for our morning coffee, and then we'll go do some shopping. But now, the right thing is for you to go to that company party."

I still don't seem convinced, so she pushes a little harder.

"Come on, you need to be a team player. Maybe you'll even meet someone there," she winks at me, and I know what she's getting at.

Ever since my last boyfriend, surfer Cody as Alisa called him, I've been on a dry spell. And, honestly, I don't see anything wrong with that. I feel good finally focusing on myself and nothing else.

"You know it's not a good idea to mix business with pleasure."

"Sometimes, it's not just a good idea, but a marvelous idea," she is still chuckling. "But I do know what you mean. Still, it wouldn't hurt you to have some fun."

"But I am having fun."

"I meant a different kind of fun."

"Oh, that," I frown.

"If you keep this up, you'll end up in a monastery."

"Oh, ha-ha, real funny," I tease, gazing at her reflection in the mirror.

"I know I'm a riot," she winks at me again. "Now, put on a little bit of mascara and some lipstick and you'll knock 'em dead."

"I don't want to knock anyone dead," I pout.

"You really are a negative Nancy this evening," she shakes her head at me. "Just stop being a smart ass and go already. Have a drink or two, mingle a little, then come home. It's just two hours of your time, but trust me, it'll be worth it."

I sigh, knowing she's probably right.

"But, what if he's there?" I suddenly ask, both of us immediately recognizing who it is I'm referring to.

"You mean your boss' boss' boss?" she chuckles, pressing her hand to her lips.

I realize she's done her nails, red this time, and it suits her perfectly. Red for a firecracker. I instinctively hide mine. Lord knows they need some attention, too, but I can't seem to get around to schedule an appointment and go have them done.

"He's a hottie, isn't he?" she asks, lifting one eyebrow.

"I don't see what that's got to do with anything," I try to evade the answer, but she knows me.

"That hot, huh?" She whistles, and it makes her sound like a construction worker on his break, hollering at a nice piece of ass. It makes me laugh. "Meaning, you'd do him."

"Seriously, Alisa..."

"Seriously, what?" she shrugs again innocently. "That's all I care about."

"And probably all he cares about is his shirt," I remind her of our unfortunate first encounter.

"Oh, shirt, shmirt," she waves her hand at me dismissively. "He's probably got tons of them. Why would he care about one? And, besides, you said he didn't mention anything when he saw you."

"That's probably because he's polite and I'm a klutz," I sigh.

"You are," she laughs again, but it's all in good fun. "I think you're safe on that one, though. He's the big man. I doubt he'd be attending a retirement party. Like, come on."

When I think about it, again – she seems right.

"Just two hours, right?" I repeat. She nods. "And coffee is on you tomorrow."

"You got it," she winks at me again, shoving her mouth with a handful of leftover chips.

"Easy, piggie," it's my turn to laugh this time.

The memory of her chomping down on those chips is still with me when I reach my office building again about an hour later. The security guy nods at me politely when I show him my ID. And I head straight towards the big banquet hall down the main hallway. The best part? It's on the ground floor.

I walk slowly, my miniature heels still clicking loudly, as if to announce my arrival. There is no one else there as I'm walking, but I hear the faint sound of music and chatter. The closer I get, the louder the noise gets, and I know it's probably a wilder party than I expected it to be.

When I reach the door, I immediately push it open. The moment I do so, a strange feeling of déjà vu washes over me. There are red balloons hanging from the ceiling, with a banner that says: We'll miss you, Dorothy!

Honestly, I wouldn't be able to pinpoint Dorothy in this room, but I try to remember Alisa's words. I'm here for one drink, to chat a little with the people I know, then head back home. This week has already been full of excitement. I honestly don't need any more of that.

I elbow my way through the crowd to the table, where I see a bowl of punch. There are half-empty bottles scattered about, but I don't like the looks of any of them.

"Pssst…" someone leans over to me, and I realize I have no idea who this guy is. "I think someone spiked the punch."

"I see," I chuckle, stepping back a little, as the guy already seemed a little tipsy and uneasy on his feet. "Maybe you should lay off it then."

"What?" he squeals. "No way!"

He proceeds to pour himself another glass, raises it at me, then disappears back in the crowd. I look around, trying to find a familiar face. I see Mr. Harrison somewhere in the distance. But he's busy talking to a few men who all have their backs turned to me.

If you can't beat them…

I sigh, turning back to the punch bowl. The pale rose liquid doesn't look very inviting, but I pour myself a glass, nonetheless. Just one drink. The moment I taste it, I realize it's not half bad.

Sipping my drink little by little, I catch myself gazing into the crowd longingly. I'm looking for a familiar face. A specifically familiar face, to be exact. A face I've seen only twice this week. A face I wished I saw more often. But I wouldn't admit it to either Alisa or myself.

When I look down, I realize my glass is empty. One more wouldn't hurt, right? So, I pour myself another drink, and continue with the inspection.

After about five minutes, I see him. The truth of my longing hits me like a tidal wave. I had no idea I would be this excited to see him. I had forgotten the rush of his presence. And, besides, he's the best-looking thing around here – that's for sure.

He's one of the people talking to Mr. Hoffman. I'm titillated, and honestly, just a little bit tipsy, but not enough to actually act on impulse and walk over there.

"Grace, right?" I hear someone call out my name, and when I turned around, I recognize the nice lady who helped me that first day.

"Sonya," I smile.

"Yes," she smiles back, obviously glad that I remembered her name. "How was your first week here?"

"Nice," I nod, trying not to look in his direction, but it's hard. It helps to know that he isn't looking my way. But, seriously, could someone really be that gorgeous? I'm not sure if that's the punch talking or it's me... not that it matters.

"... yesterday?" I hear Sonya ask, but I realize that I haven't been listening to a word she's said.

"Sorry, I didn't catch that," I touch my hand to my ear. "It's too noisy."

She leans over and repeats the question. This time, I'm focused on it.

Chapter 6

"... so, I think it'll be a good idea to just do things as we agreed, but keep them updated on any changes," Hoffman says.

"Yeah, sure," I nod, quickly.

I can't get rid of this frown. Usually, I wouldn't be caught dead at a party like this, but Dorothy knew my mother. I feel like I owe it to both of them. I squeeze the glass in my hand, then down the bitter liquid which scrapes my throat.

"As for the Livingstone account- "

"Hold that thought," I interrupt him, pointing at my empty glass. "Be right back."

I sigh, as I push my way through. I need another drink if I'm to stay here another hour. I walk over to the make-shirt bar in the corner and pour myself another scotch.

Suddenly, I feel the light touch of someone's hand on my shoulder. I twitch.

"Whoa, someone's jumpy," I turn around and see Sonya.

Luscious lips. Eyes to drown in. Curves to kill for. And yet, the thrill of the chase is gone.

"It's been a long day," I shrug, not really in the mood. "Just eager to get home."

"Does it have to be your home?" she purrs right into my ear.

I won't lie. The thought of spending another night with her is tempting. More than tempting. But I don't bite.

"Can't," I say, not even planning on offering an explanation.

She doesn't let go. "Whatever you have afterwards, you know it'll be worth it."

This is why it's not good to fuck around where you work. Something to do with not shitting where you eat, or something like that.

"I'm busy," I take a sip of my drink, and turn my back to her. Maybe she'll get the hint.

The tips of her fingers gently tap my shoulder. I sigh. Some women just don't know how to take no for an answer.

"So am I," she says, licking her upper lip seductively. That's how she got me last time. But last time I didn't have a shitload of stuff planned for the following week. Stuff I can't delegate. "Which means we both need to unwind, and what best way than- "

"Excuse me," I frown, interrupting her with a disinterested click of my lips.

I look around, looking for any other familiar face, but I see no one less annoying than the woman standing by me. Hoffman lifts his hand to call me over, but I pretend not to have seen him.

Fuck it. I'm going to finish this glass in the hallway, and then head on home. A few people nod at me as I pass by. One woman tries to grab me by the elbow. Maybe Sonya's predecessor? Not sure. I'm not even paying attention.

The reputation of a playboy still haunts me everywhere I go. The headlines are filled with my name, constantly connecting me with women I've never even met in real life. Idiots. Can't they figure out all I want is to be left alone to focus on my company? It's what I promised my father.

The memory of him hits me hard. I hate when it happens in a place like this, where I can't be alone. It was a car accident. How stupid. A car accident that took them both from me, in a single second. Mother and father gone. Forever. It took something like that for me to realize that I can't live my life like there is no tomorrow. Because sometimes, there isn't. There are consequences to everything we do. Choices haunt us. What'll always haunt me is the fact that I should have made them stay home that night, instead of going to that gala event.

Alcohol and sad memories aren't a good combination. I go outside into the hallway. It's pleasantly empty. A chill is coming from somewhere.

Then, I hear a voice. A female voice. She's giggling. She sounds happy. Almost like a child, chuckling. Curiosity takes over, and I slowly head over to where the voice is coming from. It's one of the empty offices at the end of the hallway. The door is open.

I lean inside, just to take a peek. She's with her back to me. Yellow dress. A high, messy bun. I see just her calves, nothing else. She's talking on the phone.

"... yeah..." she giggles again. The room echoes. "... maybe just a little..."

I can't help but smile, too. Her laughter is contagious. I pull a step back, into the hallway. I can't see into the room anymore. But I don't need to. I just want to listen to her voice. Just a little more of that laughter that seems so genuine. From the heart. Not a forced laughter that means you want something in return for it.

"...so hot," she says. "You wouldn't believe it..."

A boyfriend, perhaps? I take a sip of my drink. There's still half a glass left.

"... tell him that? No way, are you crazy?" she chuckles.

Now, I'm actually curious about who she's talking to, and what the conversation is about. I'm also on the verge of taking another glance, to actually see who she is. Her voice is so melodious. I mean, it made me stay here, by the door, like some weird peeping Tom. Only, I'm not even peeping. I'm listening in.

Fuck. I should just get out of here. What am I even doing?

"... Italian, I think..." she echoes again, and my ears prick up.

Could she be talking about me? I grin, despite every effort not to.

"... he's all cool and aloof, but I bet he's fire in the sack..."

I snort, pressing my hand down on my lips, stifling my laughter. So, she is talking about me. She must be. But who is she?

"... OK, I'm heading on home... I just needed to gush a little while I'm still tipsy enough to admit it..." she giggles.

I look down the hallway. It's still silent and empty. She's probably heading out of the office. If I move now, she'll know I was here. If I stay here, she'll still see me. Fuck. The only way to do this is to walk right into her.

I listen to the sound of her footsteps. Heels –they never fail to make their arrival known. Click, clack. Slow and steady.

When she's is almost at the door, I head in the same direction.

My plan works like a charm. She stumbles right onto me, and in the commotion, without even meaning to, I spill my drink all over my white shirt. That's the second one in two weeks.

"Oh, I'm..." she starts, first looking at the shirt and the stain that's spreading all over my chest, then she lifts her gaze to meet mine.

I can't believe it. It's the girl who spilled my coffee a week ago. What fucking odds.

"... so sorry..." she opens her mouth in shock, in disbelief, in total incredulity of what just happened.

Chapter 7

Grace

Oh. My. Gosh.

It's him.

I ran into him.

The guy I was just gossiping about to Alisa on the phone.

My boss' boss' boss.

The guy I already spilled coffee on. And now, some whiskey, or whatever it was he's drinking.

The world is spinning all around me. I can't believe I'm having such bad luck with this guy. I mean, seriously. Twice in two weeks. That's too much for anyone's taste.

"It's you," he suddenly says, with a flicker of a smile on his face.

"Yeah, it's me alright," I shake my head, sighing heavily, although I'm not sure what he's getting at. "The klutz."

"The klutz?" he breaks out into a full-blown smile this time.

"The coffee?" I remind him, but it's obvious he remembers me now.

"I meant, it's you, Hoffman's new assistant," he says. "But, yeah, I do remember the coffee now as well."

"I shouldn't have reminded you of it then," I still feel mortified, but at least, he's not upset. He's even smiling. Unfortunately, that made him even more desirable. More flesh and blood. Fiery and real.

"Why not?" he asks, his eyes darkening.

"Because now, you'll probably want me to buy a new shirt," I shrug, having absolutely no idea where this boldness is coming from. Someone must have spiked that punch seriously. "And your shirts probably cost half of my monthly salary."

"Two," he corrects me.

"Two months?" I gasp.

"No," he chuckles. "Two shirts."

"Crap," I mumble. "Just take it out of my salary. As for tonight, I think I've had enough partying for one evening."

"You won't be driving in this condition, will you?"

"No," I shake my head, still feeling a little tipsy.

It still has a tight grasp over me. And I know it'll all clear up by tomorrow morning. But, for now, I have to endure the heat inside of me, which keeps reminding me that I've got a super hot guy standing right in front of me, but I've already made a total fool of myself, and there's nothing I can do to fix that first impression.

"Where do you live?" he suddenly asks.

"Why?" I tilt my head at him, frowning. "You want to send your dry-cleaning check over?"

He laughs. "No. I'm offering to take you home."

My lips part in one more attack of total and utter shock. I ruined two of his shirts, and he's offering to drive me home? Holy crap.

"No, I can't accept," I tell him.

If I accept, I'll be indebted to him for life. That's not what I want.

"I couldn't in all good conscience, let you go home alone."

"I'm a big girl," I shrug, pointing at the long hallway. "And I shall take myself home, safe and sound."

"You can be a feminist all you want, when you're home in bed," he smiles. "But for now, seeing we're both on the way out, let me drive you home."

"But you've also been drinking," I squint my eyes at him, as if I'm trying to see something on him that would expose his true intentions. But, of course, there's nothing. He's just being a surprisingly nice guy. Something I never expected.

"Who says I'll be doing the driving myself?" he replies. "I have a driver."

"Well, look at you," I sing these words, and only then do I realize I'm talking to my boss' boss' boss. I should just shut my mouth, accept the ride home and be a good girl. Only, that's not who I am.

"Depends on who's doing the looking," he jokes. "Now, come on. Let's get you home."

"No, seriously, I can just call a cab. There's no need for you to go to any trouble," I'm still refusing, for some unknown reason.

Maybe it's his presence. His ghost which has been haunting me from that first encounter, and the realization that I've been yearning to see him again. Now, he's here. His gaze is so intense, my body feels electrified just by looking at him. I don't even want to know what his presence might do to me in a small, confined space of a car, with him sitting next to me. Is it a risk I'm really willing to take? On my first week at my new job?

"You're really difficult, aren't you?" I hear him say. "It's just a ride."

Maybe he's right. It is just a ride. I'm overthinking things again. As always.

As he waits, his brow arches. My gaze slides all over him. He looks so carelessly sophisticated, enough to drive any woman crazy.

"Well, OK then."

What could go wrong?

Chapter 8

Grace

We leave the building together in silence. A part of that boldness has left me, and the chilly night breeze feels good on my burning cheeks. There are a few things inside of me aching to burn, but I try not to pay attention to that need.

He walks me over to a smooth, black limo, and opens the door for me. I never thought he'd be a gentleman, but so far, everything he's done speaks in favor of one.

"Thank you," I smile, getting in. He shuts the door and enters from the other side. Just as I thought, the closeness of his body to mine is overwhelming. My breath leaves my chest in a rush,

"Where are we going?" he asks, with a smile.

In the darkness of the limo, it resembles lightning, all blinding and mysterious. I knew I'd regret letting him take me home. Regret it and welcome it at the same time. Another tidal wave of heat washes over me. That punch is still in my blood, still boiling with desire to be wicked, to be naughty. Too bad I didn't go out with Alisa. We could have picked up some guys and had some fun.

"Jackson Street," I tell him, with a barely noticeable tone of regret. "That's- "

"Downtown," he finishes my thought.

"You really enjoy interrupting people, don't you?" I frown.

"It saves us both time," he explains.

Then, he lifts his gaze towards a small window in front of us, which opened towards the driver.

"You heard the lady," he says. "Street number?"

"Forty-five," I reply. "How does it save us both time?"

"It prevents you from overly explaining things. Let's you just move on in the conversation."

"Well, I guess being the big boss man, you need to save as much time as you can."

He chuckles. "You could say that, yes. Although, no one calls me the big boss man, at least, not to my face."

"Well, you are," I state what we're both thinking. "And it sounds cute."

"Trust me, in the corporate world, the last thing you want to be is cute," he shakes his head, but that smile is still there. "If you're a man."

"You're saying it works differently for a woman?" I tease, enjoying the banter.

"Always," he nods, importantly. "And don't even try to convince me otherwise, because I won't buy it."

I laugh. "OK, I won't."

"Thank you," he smiles. "My drink ended up on my shirt again, but at least I can tell everyone that I got a woman to agree with what I was saying."

"That doesn't happen very often?" My eyes flare up.

Just listening to his luscious voice is enough. It makes me relax on an unconscious level, and I know a part of me will be sad when I get home, because I'll have to leave his limo. And yet, it feels like tonight could be the start of something, something I'm not even sure what exactly it is or could be, but I want it. I want everything he has to give, and it's probably the punch talking, but I'd even agree to a one-night stand with him.

Technically, I don't work for him. Seeing him that first day on the job was just a coincidence. Mr. Hoffman said it himself, he'd be taking up those documents if it weren't for his daughter's birthday. Meaning, I probably won't be doing much traveling to the twenty-second floor. Thank goodness for that.

That also means that I might put this punch to good use and maybe be a little more flirtatious. Not like I'm in the limo of a billionaire every single evening, right?

"You don't strike me as the kind of guy who couldn't get a woman to agree with him," I continue, teasing him on purpose, trying the limits and seeing how far he would let me go. And the more I do it, the more fun it is.

"I never said that," he shakes his head, leaning back into the leather seat, which cringes underneath his weight.

I look around, and a naughty idea pops up. There's more than enough room here for a hot quickie, and we could totally-

"Just saying it's generally a difficult thing to do," he finishes his thought, interrupting mine.

"That is true," I nod, stealing yet another moment to look at him greedily.

His savage beauty is incomparable, his fine features sculpted perfectly. He is the kind of man that makes you look not twice, but twice and then a third time that would never end.

"But it also depends on the woman," I lean back as well, getting more comfortable.

The limo glides so peacefully, I can't even tell we're moving. Instead, I feel like we're stuck in some parallel universe, where such a thing, as me getting a ride home from the top boss, was actually a possibility. As if the lines between fantasy and reality are blurred, and I'm allowed to do anything, to try anything, because none of it will matter in the morning. It will be like it never happened.

"It depends on the person, really," he explains. "Reason is something both men and women possess. Then, we like to pretend like someone has more or less of it when we make a mistake."

"But some mistakes are so much fun," I chuckle.

"They certainly are," he joins in. "That's why we keep doing them, isn't that so?"

The way he speaks, the way he laughs, even the way he looks at things, it all reveals a powerful magnate who can get whatever he wants at the snap of his fingers. I see a rakish curl fall over his forehead, and my fingers tingle with the desire to touch it, to brush it back.

Suddenly, I see him leaning over to me. His gaze is intense, scorching hot. My lips part, and a violent rush of goosebumps explodes all throughout my body. He leans in more, his right arm stretching, as if to land right on my waist.

Impatiently, I wait, but he is too slow. I pull myself closer to him, our lips almost touching. The moment is sinfully right. I just need to move a few inches closer and that would be enough. But I want him to do it. So, I close my eyes, waiting. Anticipating. Eager and yearning.

A moment passes by. Nothing happens. Another. Then another.

I open my eyes, and I realize he's pulled away, back onto his seat, looking at me, as if he's just seen a ghost.

Oh... my... gosh... He wasn't even planning on kissing me...

"I... uhm... just wanted to get my lighter from the side pocket, over there," he says confused, pointing somewhere to my side, but I'm too mortified to pay any attention to that.

This is strike three. If I don't die right now of complete and utter embarrassment, I don't think I ever will. The darkness inside the limo isn't complete, but hopefully it's enough to hide my burning cheeks.

"Sorry, I..." I apologize, but there's nothing to apologize for, and also, there's nothing to say.

I'm just waiting for this ride to be over, so I can slither on into my bed and hide underneath the covers, never to go out into the world again.

"No, I'm sorry, I..." he repeats the same thing, us both aware of how stupid it sounds.

"It's OK," I end this cycle of stupid statements, regaining a little bit of confidence as well as my senses.

Also, I doubt I'll ever be drinking punch again.

"It's not you, it's just..." he tries to make it better, but that's an impossible feat.

"It's fine, I understand," I mutter more to myself than to him, trying not to look in his direction. That would only make my cheeks flare up even more, and that's the last thing I need right now.

Finally, the limo stops and the privacy window that separated us from the driver rolls down.

"We're here, Mr. Barbati," he says.

Thank Heavens. Some merciful force in the universe saw my embarrassment and decided that enough is enough. I can run on home.

"Thank you for the ride, Mr. Barbati," I say as officially as I can muster, as if none of that previous talk and fun banter ever happened.

If I'm to forget this mishap, then I must forget the entire evening. I can't stop in the middle. It has to be all the way.

"You're welcome, ah... sorry, I forgot your name."

"Grace Hensley."

Having to repeat my name on top of everything truly makes this night a total miss. I grab at the door to push it open, eager to get out and get away.

"Good night," I hastily add to my second introduction, then I slam the door behind me.

Shaking with humiliation and anger mostly at myself, I run up the stairs, hoping to find Alisa awake.

Chapter 9

Grace

"Come on, come on, rise and shine!"

I hear Alisa's voice, but I pretend not to. The hangover that I feel in the back of my head is less than I thought it would be, so I'm grateful for that courtesy. Still, I hide underneath the covers, refusing to answer.

"Come on, I know you're not sleeping," she says, sitting on the bed, as I feel the gentle commotion.

"I'm dead to the world," I manage to mumble.

She chuckles. "Well, after last night, I thought you would say that. But, trust me, I have such a day planed for us, that will make you forget all about that prick."

Prick.

I have to say, she managed to make me smile. As always.

"So, I'll go make us some coffee, and you, darling, will go and take a shower in the meantime. I want you nice and clean today. Not a single memory of last night."

"Easier said than done," I speak up from underneath the covers, sounding like I'm hiding inside a deep, dark cave. It's actually where I'd rather be now, instead of negotiating the conditions of my entry into the world again.

"Yeah, yeah," she gets up from the bed. "You've got fifteen minutes of privacy, then I'm barging into the shower and scrubbing you down myself."

I hear her footsteps disappearing out from my bedroom. It's silent once more. I don't want to get up. I really don't. All I think about is how I waited for him to kiss me, and how stupid I must have looked. What an idiot. I can't even imagine what he must think of me.

I grip at the covers even more desperately. I just want to be left alone to wallow in misery, but I know Alisa won't allow that. Maybe telling her all about it was a mistake. Only, she'd take one look at me today and know that something was wrong. We've been friends for far too long for her to miss something like this.

I sigh loudly, but there is no relief in it. I doubt there ever will be again, especially if I find myself in the same room with Rocco Barbati. Why does he have to have such a fuckable name? Everything about him screams hot and spicy, and I just want a taste.

"I don't hear the water running!" Alisa shouts from the kitchen.

"Fine, fine…" I stick out my tongue to no one really, but the childishly defiant motion makes me feel a little better, and I finally peek from underneath the covers.

Everything is bright. Too bright. Alisa has pushed the curtains to the side. There's too much sun. Too much commotion. Too much life. There's too much of everything this morning.

I take a long, hot shower, surprised by the effects of it. Refreshed, I actually feel a little better now, as if the very residue of last night was finally washed off of me. Still in my robe, I make my way to the kitchen. Alisa is seated at our small, round table. There's a cup of coffee in front of her, and one opposite her. She's got her phone in her hand, but the moment I walk in, she puts it down respectfully. We both do it when talking to each other, finding people who stare at their phones while conversing with people face to face rude.

"Glad to see you're back among the living," she smiles.

"Barely," I snort, sitting down, and enveloping the cup with both hands. The very smell reminds me how much I need a caffeine pick me up this morning.

"So, he's not into you. Big deal," she frowns, reminding me of everything I want to forget. But tough luck.

That's just how your brain works. If you want to remember something, you have to take an actual effort at doing so. On the other hand, when you want to forget about something and never think of it again, suddenly your brain seems to be your enemy and not your friend.

Right now, that's the relationship we have, as it keeps showing me only Rocco Barbati and nothing else.

"It's not just that, Alisa," I shake my head, with a heavy sigh, trying to think of anything other than him. Cute kittens. Nuns dancing the can-can. Werewolves. Anything really. But nothing works.

"I have made a fool of myself in front of that man one too many times. Two too many times. Three times. Yes, three times."

Alisa laughs melodiously at my words. Hell, I'm happy that at least someone is having fun with this, because I sure am not.

"I'm serious," I try not to smile, but her laughter is contagious. "I was kinda hoping we could have some no strings attached, mind blowing sex, but that's not happening."

"Look at you, with your big expectations," she winks at me.

"Well, you know how things are," I sigh. "I'm really not interested in a relationship. I have no idea where I'd fit it in, especially with this new job. And, even if I was looking for something serious, something-
"

"Something along the lines of happily ever after?" she interrupts temptingly.

"Yeah, even if I was looking for something like that, I wouldn't get that from someone like Rocco. I mean, come on. I doubt the guy's capable of committing to anything more than ordering something at a restaurant and then actually eating it. That's as far as his commitment stretches. But a night of wild passion? That might be something I'm interested in."

We exchange a meaningful glance, then we both burst out into loud laughter. I love having her as my best friend. No one has ever understood me better than she has, and no one has ever dared to offer me stark contrasting opinions without fear. That's what makes her a good friend. If your dress makes you fat, you can rest assured that she won't let you go out of the apartment wearing it. And that's what I value in people. Honesty.

"OK, Miss. Modesty," she jokes. "Let's forget about Italian studs and focus on just the two of us today."

"I'd really like that," I smile back, knowing that this probably won't be quite possible, but I'm willing to try. "What did you have in mind?"

"First, we'll go spend some money."

"Money we still haven't earned, huh?"

Another bout of laughter explodes, and I already feel much better than half an hour ago. Everyone should have an Alisa in their lives to make up for all the bad shit that happens to them on a daily basis.

"Then, we'll spend the afternoon at that place you've been dying to try out."

"Wait, you don't mean to tell me..." I gasp, leaning over to her.

"Yes, I totally do," she beams at me. "I booked us the afternoon at Dr. Feelgood Spa."

"I can't believe you did that," I shake my head at her, totally incredulous.

Dr. Feelgood Spa is one of the most expensive places in the city, if not the most expensive. Sure, I've been dying to try it out, but not at the expense of breaking the bank. I've been waiting for the right reason to celebrate, and it seems that Alisa has made that decision for me. Sometimes, I think she knows me better than I know myself. That's the best part about best friends.

"You deserve it," she tells me, grinning from ear to ear. "I deserve it, too. So, why don't we pamper ourselves?"

While she does make a lot of sense, as always, the thing is that this place cost an arm and a leg. It's something girls like us can save for, and then indulge in maybe once or twice a year. Never on a regular basis.

"I'm paying you back for this," I decide to accept only under this condition.

"No, you aren't. It'll be your treat next time," she corrects me. "Or you can take me to that new French restaurant that just opened."

"So, that was your devious plan all along," I laugh. "I knew you were hiding something."

"You know me," she winks, then proceeds to take a sip of her coffee.

"Oh, I do need some pampering after the week I've had," I shake my head, still with occasional images of what a fool I've been.

The coffee stain on that shirt. How his chest muscles felt underneath my touch. How stupid I must have appeared. My eyebrows furrow in agony. Will I ever be able to get that image out of my mind and fully focus on something else?

"I still think you're blowing it way out of proportion," she continues to calm me down, and I appreciate her patience with me, as always. She never has a problem repeating something several times, in order for me to finally accept it.

"I'd like to believe that," I sigh. "Hopefully, by the end of the day I will."

We spend the next few hours shopping, although once again, I barely found anything I liked. Alisa, on the other hand, always returns from our shopping trips with bags and bags of clothes, which she is barely able to stuff in her wardrobe. But, that's never been an issue for her. She's the type to simply get a new, bigger wardrobe instead of shopping less.

We find ourselves in front of Dr. Feelgood Spa at the designated time. Alisa walks in first, while I take my time enjoying the interior with lush, bright red silks hanging from the doorway and the ceiling. There are golden framed, elegant looking sofas and armchairs, which are just beckoning you to lounge, resting on the golden bejeweled pillows.

I hear the sound of birds chirping, and I immediately turn back at the doorway, but it's closed. For a moment, I wonder how strange it is to hear that sound, especially seeing we're in the very center of the city, bustling with life and the sounds of civilization.

Then, I realize the chirping isn't coming from outside, but rather from inside. There are four cages hanging in all four corners of the reception room. Inside each cage, two yellow canary birds are jumping cheerfully, chatting with each other in their sweet-sounding language.

Adding to the serenity and the beauty of the place are two fountains, and if you close your eyes, you could imagine yourself being lost in some wonderful forest. The only thing taking away from that sensation is the music coming in from speakers which could not be pinpointed. Although the music isn't intrusive, for me personally, the chirping and the sound of running water would be enough for an oasis of peace.

I watch as Alisa walks over to the perfectly dolled up lady who works at the reception. Her dark auburn hair is tied sleekly backwards, coming together into a smooth ballerina bun. Her cat eye is on spot and her dark plum lipstick only adds to her the mystery she is trying to create with her look.

"Welcome, ladies," she beams at us. "How may I help you?"

Alisa takes over, and I let her. I just hope this won't cost her an arm and a leg. Because everyone knows that Dr. Feelgood Spa isn't for everyone. Luxurious and offering anything you could possibly imagine when it comes to rest and relaxation, this spa place is only for those who can afford it. Or, in our case, for those who will just get a skim off the top, because that is how much we personally can afford. Still, it should be enough to feel pretty and privileged.

"This is our menu, ladies," the girl slides two menus with a pearly, silver finish.

I enjoy reading the names. Milk and honey bath. Berry beautiful woman. Fine-apple pineapple masks and baths. I chuckle at the Mud-dle cuddle in the warrior woman package.

"What do you like?" Alisa asks me.

"Oh, I'm fine with any of these," I shrug, pretending that I haven't seen the sky-high prices of this place. "As long as we do it together."

"Well, we have this couples' package," the girl slides her red, manicured finger on my menu and stops at the couples' package. "And you also get a discount there. It's not two for one, but almost."

I glance over at Alisa. We smile at each other.

"Perfect," we both say at the same time.

About half an hour later, we're sitting in pedicure chairs, one next to the other. We've both got cucumber masks on, and the foot massage that preceded the pedicure was to die for. We're both silent, when I suddenly hear parts of the conversation between the girls sitting opposite us.

"... he's hot hot..." one of them says.

"Aren't all Italians?" the other one adds, with a giggle.

At the mention of the word Italian, my ears prick up.

"Only if they're named Rocco Barbati," the first one says again, and they burst into another chuckle. "A friend of mine slept with him, and she says he's a beast..."

I turn to Alisa, and I see that one of the cucumbers has already fallen from her eyes. Mine were both gone by this point. She gives me a meaningful glance, with a raised eyebrow. I just shake my head softly at her. She presses her lips tightly together, probably so she wouldn't burst out chuckling.

I sigh, closing my eyes again. It seems it's impossible to escape the mention of this guy's name.

Chapter 10

Rocco

Mondays are usually hectic enough, without having someone constantly on your mind. All morning, people keep coming in and out of my office, as if Veronica, my secretary, purposely scheduled all my appointments for today.

I still need those documents delivered to me signed and sealed, and I can't do anything without them. A whole shitload of emails is waiting for my reply, and I haven't even opened my email account this morning.

"Veronica?" I press the button to call her, while still seated at my desk.

"Yes, Mr. Barbati?" she immediately replies.

She's not what you'd expect of a secretary. She isn't hot by any standards. Those glasses have just slightly thicker lenses than they should. Her sweaters are always buttoned up all the way to her throat. She's been the butt of many jokes, but one thing is for sure. I wouldn't change her for any other hot piece of ass secretary in the world. She gets the job done better than any other girl at the phone I've seen. As long as she keeps doing her job that way, she can dress and look any way she wants.

"Do I have anything scheduled for the next hour?"

An idea suddenly pops up. Crazy. But I know that's the only way to get her out of my mind – to get her in front of me.

"Um, no, I don't think so, Mr. Barbati," she says. "But, let me double check… no. Your next appointment is at 2 o'clock with Mr.- "

"Yes, it's Colton, I remember."

"Yes, Mr. Colton," she confirms, her voice a perfect tonality of politeness and respectability.

"Thanks, Veronica."

"You're welcome, Mr. Barbati."

I let go of the button, leaning more into the leather chair. The big window lets in enough light. It's a great day. Too great to spend it inside, especially during lunch time. And, I haven't even had breakfast this morning, rushing out of my place and right over here. My stomach reminds me of that with a slight rumble.

That same idea from before pops to mind again. I don't remember the last time I had lunch outside, during the work week, unless it was a business meeting. I also haven't taken out my little black book in ages. Well, actually, in years. Two years. Ever since... it happened.

The little black book went into oblivion. Not like I needed it, anyway. Veronica has been doing a very good job of keeping jobless heiresses out of my hair while I'm here. And I've been doing that same job keeping myself occupied at home, too. I haven't been attending many social events, and people understood. Death in the family is a good excuse to get out of the spotlight.

But now, maybe it's time to slowly start getting back out there. And I've got just the right person to help me ease the transition.

I press the buzzer again.

"Veronica?"

"Yes, Mr. Barbati?" Her voice is always agreeable, and that was actually one of the reasons why I hired her in the first place. Can't have your secretary screeching at someone over the phone.

"Get me Hoffman's assistant on the phone, please."

"Right away, Mr. Barbati."

I always intend to tell her that she needs to tone it down with the Mr. Barbati, but I guess if she did, it wouldn't be her.

I stay on the line, waiting to be connected. It takes only a few seconds for Veronica to work her magic.

"Hello, this is Grace Hensley, Mr. Hoffman's assistant, how may I help you?"

"You could have lunch with me," I can't resist just laying it out there.

"Um..." she sounds confused. I can imagine her blushing like that night inside my limo. "Who is this?"

A part of me is offended. That manly, ego part that expects every girl to recognize me instantly just by hearing my breath. Only, she's heard my voice and hasn't responded as she was supposed to, as I've expected her to. I calm down my bruised ego easily.

"This is Rocco." Then, I added, out of sheer pleasure. "Rocco Barbati."

"Oh, Mr. Barbati," she repeats flatly. There is no emotion in that voice while she repeats my name.

A strange tickle passes through my groin. I wonder what she would sound saying my first name, and maybe adding a few moans to it. A weird sensation washes over me, travelling down, where very fee sensations have been headed lately. I'm glad to hear that everything is working well down there even after this long time of inactivity.

"After what we've been through, I should think Rocco is fine," I chuckle.

She doesn't. I hear her breathing, steady and maybe a little agitated. But, curious. I've seen those eyes. I've seen the fire inside them. And she wanted me to kiss her that night. That much was obvious.

Only, I don't kiss drunk girls. Nor do I do anything with them. Bad shit could come of it, and I don't even want to risk it. Unless the whole evening started off that way, getting drunk together and then leading to hot, raw sex. Otherwise, taking a drunk girl home and kissing her, or anything else, is out of the question.

"I um... I already apologized," she finally says, disappointing me in the process.

Did I sound like I was calling to get her to apologize again? I hope not. Unless she aimed to apologize using this pretty mouth of hers in some other way than speaking. The thought tickles my groin even further.

"I didn't say that to require another apology," I reply, knowing that I sound too official, but her voice isn't all that welcoming.

Maybe she's offended I didn't try anything? Well, I'll be glad to correct that, if only she lets me.

"I was just hoping you'd join me for lunch," I explain.

This isn't my type of a game. I don't take out girls to lunch. Never did. It's always been only dinner, with the intention of fucking. They were all aware of this ahead of time, just so there was no confusion. I hate confusion. I hate false expectations.

Also, dating takes too much time, too much effort, and it barely gets you anything in return, apart from sex. So, I've been handling my love life like I handle my business. Straight to the point. No side-tracking. In and out, and we're done, with everyone getting exactly what they wanted and what they expected out of this mutually beneficial transaction.

"Lunch?" she repeats, as if she doesn't know what it means. "You're inviting me to lunch?"

"Yes, I believe that's what I said," I smile. "Hoffman lets you have your lunch break, doesn't he?"

"Yes..."

"Because, if he doesn't, I'll have to have a talk with him," I continue still joking, but I don't hear much response on the other side, apart from some more mysterious silence.

Usually, girls are gushing to talk to me. I can't get a word in from them squealing. Grace, it seems, is very different.

"Of course, he does," she informs me, almost like Veronica when she's scheduling a meeting. She's nice and polite, but you know she's only talking to you because it's her job.

"Then, the only question is whether you're hungry."

"Well..." she sighs, and that's never a good sign. It's an unexpected sign, too. Am I a reason to sigh to her? "I do appreciate your offer, Mr.

Barbati, I really do. But I'm swamped with work these days, and I won't be leaving my desk for lunch."

I frown. It's her second week at work. Could Hoffman really be drilling her so much, right from the beginning? That doesn't seem like him.

"You plan on staying hungry then?" I take another shot.

"I brought food from home, so I won't be hungry."

And it's another miss. I should be upset. That's the reasonable reaction in this situation, right? I mean, I've never been in one. I've never had a girl say no to lunch or dinner with me. Or anything, really. But she is. Grace Hensley is actually saying no to me using the oldest excuse in the book. She's busy.

The funniest part? I have no idea what to say to that. I just keep grinning, because I'm having so much fun with this girl, and she doesn't even know it. If she thinks one no is enough for me to stop hounding her, then she's got another thing coming.

"Now, if you don't need me or Mr. Hoffman for anything else, Mr. Barbati, I have to get back to work, or I won't even have time to eat at my desk."

She says it with such ease, as if she herself is enjoying saying no.

"I understand, Grace," I make sure to say her name. "And, please, drop the Mr. I never liked it."

"But it's your name," she says, and I can't resist the urge to laugh.

"That it is," I nod more to myself than to her.

"Enjoy your lunch, Mr. Barbati," she adds, then hangs up.

She actually hangs up on me. I'm still with the phone in my hand. My lips are parted, in a soundless letter A.

Oh, Grace. The chase is on. You just don't know it yet.

Chapter 11

Grace

When I hang up the phone, I'm still a bit shaken. The very sound of his voice is enough to make me shiver with all sorts of thoughts and ideas. And then, I remember everything that's happened between us, and this shivering becomes even stronger.

He called. He actually called me and invited me out to lunch. I have to admit, I wasn't expecting that. Not in a million years. I thought the events that took place were enough to keep us apart, because obviously, the universe doesn't want us together in any shape or form. And yet, we both seem to be pushing for the opposite. Only, now it's more him than me.

I know what Alisa would have said. I should have said yes, accepted it, apologized again, and let it all go, let it all take a natural course.

But I can't. Nothing about this thing, whatever it is, has been going the right way, and it's probably for the best that nothing continues. We should just remain professional. Whenever we see each other, we should just pretend like nothing else happened, and everything will be OK.

I try to focus on work, but it's hard. I just seem to stare at the laptop screen in front of me, and every time I read something, I have to reread it, because I have absolutely no idea what it was about. So, focus is off the table for the day.

"Grace?" I pick up the phone and hear Mr. Hoffman's voice. "Could you please come to my office."

"Right away," I reply, jumping at the opportunity to do something more productive, than keep rereading the same text for a whole hour and not memorizing anything from it.

When I enter his office, he immediately tells me to sit down, and proceeds to ask my opinion regarding the Bateman project. Somehow, probably because I don't want to get fired or present myself as an incompetent assistant, I am finally able to focus, and we spend the next two hours productively.

"Thanks for the input, Grace," he smiles at me, then checks his watch. "Sorry about making you skip your lunch break."

"It's OK," I smile back, gathering a few of the papers he's handed me over the past two hours. "It's my job, after all."

"While that is true, I still don't want you to drop dead from hunger," he laughs.

"No fear of that ever happening," I assure him. "I always have a protein candy bar in my bag, just for such emergencies. Besides, I've been meaning to stay at my desk and finish some of the reports you've asked me to."

"But those are for the end of the week," he says, almost surprised that I chose to do something before the actual deadline.

"I know," I nod. "I just like to start on my things early, just in case something pops up later."

"And, how old are you, Grace? Twenty something?" His head is tilted, as if he's still trying to figure me out and can't believe I'm saying those very same words which are leaving my lips.

"Twenty-five," I reply, not sure if in this case it will work against me or for me. But, then again, he's hired me. He must know my age.

"I thought so," he nods. "Still, a very wise and 'old' way of thinking," he adds, giving finger quotation marks to the word old. I chuckle at his performance. "It's so difficult to find someone so conscientious as you."

"I'm just doing my job."

"And you're doing it very well."

"I appreciate your words very much, Mr. Hoffman," I thank him, truly grateful to be here.

"Now, go and eat something, I don't want anyone to accuse me of starving my staff."

We both chuckle at his words. I nod, then walk out of his office and back over to my desk. I eat the ham and cheese sandwich Alisa made me for lunch. That stinky cheese is an extra touch I wasn't expecting. But, then again, today seems to be the day when many unexpected things happen.

I wolf down the whole thing, then make myself a coffee, and miraculously, that streak of focus is still with me. I spend the rest of the afternoon productively, only stopping to answer a call from Alisa, who just wanted to ask me what she should order for dinner. My choice for this evening was Chinese, and I knew she'd agree with it.

Eventually, I bring my working day to an end, and once I check to see if my desk is left all nice and tidy, I switch off my computer and head over to the elevators. The mere thought of them still makes me nauseous. But I've been following Sonya's advice. I don't look down. If possible, that is if no one else is there with me, I just close my eyes and listen to the pinging sounds. Once the door opens, I rush out and take a deep breath.

I have to admit, having done it fifty times now has made it just a little less uncomfortable, although still not pleasant. Hopefully, one day I'll be able to ride up and down this elevator and not have that knot in my stomach.

For now, that knot is here, as I'm calling for the elevator. I hear distant chatter, which means people are still here. I'm among the first ones to head home today. Not a usual sight, though. I figured that it was my first week on the job. It wouldn't look good if I'm the first one to leave. So, I made sure to leave among the last ones. Today, however, I feel like I wouldn't do more than I've already done anyway.

I wait for the elevator patiently, soothing that feeling of unpleasantness in my gut. I doubt this feeling will ever go away, especially with this stupid floor. But I've somehow come to terms with it. I just don't look down. I press the button I need, and I close my eyes. Now, I don't care even if there are people inside the elevator with me. I still close my eyes, and I count the precious seconds until the door opens again and I rush outside.

But today I feel not only unpleasant about my usual elevator ride, but also happy that despite everything, I managed to have a productive day. My stomach rumbles at the thought of some delicious Chinese food with my best friend. Who needs guys anyway? They just complicate everything. They just make everything a mess. They just...

... like being in the right place at the right time.

Like now, when the door to the elevator opens wide, and I see Rocco inside.

Chapter 12

Grace

His face lights up when he sees me, and I have to admit, who wouldn't love to have such an effect on a man?

My knees go weak just at the sight of him. But I have to be cautious. If I fall for him, then I'm doomed. Absolutely doomed. And that's the last thing I need. So, I can't get close to him in any way. In fact, I need to do the exact opposite. I have to stay as far away from him as possible, so I wouldn't be this attracted to him. I have to build up some kind of immunity to his charm, if such a thing is even possible. Actually, I doubt that the attraction would diminish. I would just stop thinking about him so often... maybe.

"Going down?" he says cheekily, holding the door, noticing that I haven't moved.

"I should be, yes," I nod, but I still don't move.

"You obviously don't do many things you should be doing, like that lunch with me today."

I smile, despite the growing uneasiness in my stomach. Now, the reason for that knot is twofold. It's not only the elevator. It's also the man inside.

The easiest thing to do would be to just let him go down on his own and wait for the next elevator. Or maybe even walk down. But I can't. I can't stop staring back at him, and I realize with each passing moment that every time I see him, he is more striking, more handsome, more irresistible. Is such a thing even possible? Obviously yes.

Besides, this building belongs to him. I can't avoid him for the rest of my time here, which I hope will be long and prosperous. I have to get used to his presence. I have to become unaffected by his gorgeous looks.

"No hard feelings," he says with that same mischievous smile. "In fact, I admire that in a woman, to be able to fully focus on work and give it her all."

"Thank you," I reply, still a little confused, but happy that the conversation takes on a different course.

"Now, why don't you come on in," he suggests, his hand still on the door, provocatively. "There's plenty of room for both of us."

I take a step, but then I see the floor and him standing on it. I see all the wires, the tubes, the silver metal which is separating me from life and certain death.

I immediately pull back, shaking my head. He looks at me, a little confused, but then there is a spark of recognition, of memory.

"You get dizzy in elevators," he suddenly remembers.

I lift my brow in surprise, but I don't let it show. So, he remembers I hate these glass monsters – so what?

"Only these with glass floors," I explain, pointing at his feet.

"I guess I wasn't thinking when I had these installed," he says with a strange note of regret in his voice, as if he really wouldn't have them set up this way if he had known people wouldn't feel comfortable inside of them.

"No one else seems to have a problem with them," I shrug, to show him that he couldn't have predicted me coming here and getting all worked up over his elevators.

"Honestly, I wouldn't care if anyone else had a problem with them."

Was that a compliment? Did I hear that right?

But I need to stay focused. Just as I'm about to say that I can't risk entering the elevator with him inside, he offers his other hand to me.

"Come," he smiles, his voice resonant and strong. "I promise to keep you safe."

My brain lurches into thought mode. What is he doing? Why is he saying all this? What does he want to achieve? So many questions, but no answers.

I feel his gaze all over me, scanning my profile, my face, waiting for my reaction. That makes both of us. He doesn't look away for even a single second. Waiting.

It doesn't take me long to make up my mind. Without even thinking, I take his hand. Sure, I might throw up all over him, but I suppose he's already gotten used to having his shirts destroyed by me spilling things on him. This would simply be lucky number three.

He takes a step back to allow me in. My hand in his feels electrifying. Strange awareness prickles all over my skin, and I feel like all my senses are heightened. This is horrible. I can't look down. I can't look at him. Where the heck am I supposed to look at?

I try to calm myself down, but that's already a lost cause. The sexual magnetism this man exudes is undeniable. I can feel it even without touching him. I shift restlessly on my feet, as if not touching the floor would make it better.

He presses the button and the door closes. The elevator slowly starts its descent. I barely feel it. But I know that, if I look down, I will be nauseous. I'm immediately regretting this decision.

Then, he smiles at me, and steps closer. He takes my other hand into his.

"Close your eyes," he whispers.

Not knowing what else to do, I follow his command.

"There was this beach I went to once," he starts speaking softly. "The waves were crashing against the shore, and a few seagulls croaked in the distance…"

"Croaked?" I open one eye to look at his serious face. "Seagulls don't croak. Frogs do."

He chuckles immediately, shaking his head. "Are you telling the story here? Close your eyes."

I smile, doing again as he says.

"The palm trees were swaying in the wind… There was not a single person around, just me… soaking up the sunset, and all the colors that seemed to explode on the horizon before me... I was walking barefoot, and I could feel the sand between my webbed toes..."

"Wait, what?" I open both my eyes again. "Did you say webbed toes?"

"Just making sure you're listening," he laughs with a sound that washes over me in a seductive rhythm. "I don't really have webbed feet."

"Well, how can I be sure of that now?" I tease, not even realizing how easily he has pulled me into his game. Not only did I welcome it, but I was also enjoying it as well.

"Want me to take off my shoes and socks right here, right now?" he offers.

"Oh, God no!" I can't hide my smile.

At that moment, I hear the familiar ping noise and the door slides open. I pull my hands away from him, as if I've been burned. Snatch them away, even. Then, I rush out of the elevator. He slowly walks out and joins me on the way through the main entrance. I try to focus on the clicking sound of my short heels against the tiled flooring.

"Thanks," I say, still a little bewildered and under the impression of what just happened. "That was nice... what you did."

"Despite what you may think, I'm a pretty decent guy," he replies to the gentle quiver inside my stomach.

"I never said you weren't."

"You didn't have to," he explains with a helpless shrug. "It was implied."

I don't know what to say to that. So, I remain quiet, hoping that he will extract the meaning he wants out of it.

"Well..." I say once we're out of the building. "I parked across the street."

He frowns at me. "We do have an underground parking, you know?"

"I know, but no one asked if I needed a spot and I didn't inquire on how to go about getting one," I shrug. "Not that it matters."

"Of course, it matters," he shakes his head, obviously a bit agitated. "I'll look into it first thing tomorrow morning, and you'll get your spot."

"No, seriously, it's fine," I assure him. "I can just park there. It's totally fine."

"Grace…" he says suddenly. "You can't be so nice."

I chuckle at his words. "Why not?"

"Because you won't get what you want."

"How do you know I'm not getting what I want?" I tilt my head a little, amused by the conversation. I don't even feel that embarrassment from before.

"If you were, you'd be agreeing to lunch with me," he flashes a smile to die for. "Or, now that the lunch offer is off the table, you could agree to a dinner."

His amusement is contagious. And it seems that our fun only progresses.

"I um, actually have plans already," I smile, shrugging helplessly.

"May I know with whom?" he asks so naturally that I'm not even shocked at his question.

"Doesn't that go out of the confines of employee employer?"

"It does," he nods, matter-of-factly. "Because it's not an employee employer question. And, besides, we're out of working hours now. So, whatever we talk about is considered friendly banter."

"Is it now?" I can't resist the urge to laugh.

He takes a step closer to me now. I can smell his cologne. Strong and overpowering. Just like him.

"You are avoiding my question," he reminds me.

I would reply, only my thoughts are running away from me. But I don't say any of that out loud.

"Well, if you must know, my roommate is waiting for me at home. She ordered Chinese," I explain, opting for the truth instead of making him believe I'm with someone.

Why would I? Not like anything would happen. He probably just feels bad about pulling away in the limo and wants to feel better about himself by taking me out to dinner or lunch or whatever. Well, I'm no-one's charity case. Not even his. I got his message loud and clear.

"If she is your roommate, then she won't mind you standing her up."

"No, that's exactly why she would mind," I correct him. "I stand up people I don't know or people I don't care about. As for people I do care about, I make sure that their feelings are not hurt by anything I do. And, if I say I'm going to do something, I damn right do it."

My little monologue ends with my heart rushing and my cheeks blushing. But, from the look of it, I managed to get my message across.

"I bid you good night, Mr. Barbati," I smile, turning my back to him before he even has the chance to reply, and I start walking away from him.

"It's..." he starts but doesn't finish his sentence.

I know he's watching me as I cross the street and get over to my car.

Let him. That's all he can do.

Chapter 13

Rocco

This is not me. This is so not me. This guy, sitting in his car, watching a building. Waiting. Like a stalker.

No. A stalker would be someone who would use his connections and the fact that he was her boss, to find out everything there is to know about her. And I do mean everything. Honestly, I'd rather have her tell me all that herself. That's the point.

I check my watch. It's a Rolex my father gave me as a present, when I was just twenty years old. It was supposed to remind me that coming from wealth shouldn't make me take things for granted. I didn't really get the idea behind it. You want someone to appreciate what they have, but you gift them a super expensive watch that about two percent of the population can afford? Makes no sense.

Only, now it somehow does. It reminds me of family values, of the fact that he rose from rags to riches, and it was his backing that helped me expand our business into what it is today. Our business. It will always be our business. Family business.

She should have been home by now. I didn't want to catch her at the office. She would probably blow me off again, like yesterday.

I remember how she shivered in the elevator. Her hands were soft. A little clammy. But, she was still unafraid to that extent that she wouldn't allow herself to be pushed around, even as a joke. Not that it was my intention.

It's fun trying to find out where her boundaries are. There is just something about her that's different. It could be just the fact that she won't fall for me just like that, like all the others. I'm used to just pointing at a girl and she'd walk over to me, ready to do whatever I want. It's nice and all, but it gets boring. I miss the thrill of the hunt. And Grace Hensley seems to be the perfect prey.

Another fifteen minutes pass, and I finally see her car approaching. She parks right in front of the building. It takes her five minutes to get out of the car. What could she be doing? I'm surprised to realize that I actually care.

By the time she's out of the car, I'm already across the street, walking over to her. She lowers her head to look for the keys in her bag, and she jumps when she lifts her gaze to meet mine. Her body takes a defensive stance, and I know if she doesn't recognize me immediately, I might end up with a punch on the nose.

"Rocco!" she gasps, dropping the keys to the ground.

I laugh, bending first to reach for them, then offering her what she almost lost. At least it's not a punch on the nose. This I can handle.

"It's nice to know that you do know my first name," I chuckle.

"What.. what are you doing here?" she asks, her eyes wide like a doe's.

I'm looking straight at her, and apart from that initial shock and surprise, I see nothing else. She won't give anything else away. The memory of her hand in mine ripples through my chest and shoots down. South. Way down south.

I want to get closer to her, put my hand on the small of her back and steer her towards me, since she doesn't seem to know the way. Or maybe, she knew the way, but lost herself somehow.

"Waiting for you, of course," I explain.

"Why?"

She sucks in a deep breath, and regret hits me like a ton of bricks. I should have just kissed her in the limo. I would have saved myself all this headache and effort. But also the thrill wouldn't be here. Now, she's playing hard to get, and I'm more than eager to play the hunter.

"Because you owe me a dinner," I say.

The street around us is empty. I could pull her towards me right here and kiss her breathless. She wouldn't know what hit her. But now I don't want it to happen so quickly. I want her to wait, just like I've been waiting these few days. I want her to beg.

She frowns. Her lips pout just a little, making them even more kissable.

"Has it occurred to you that maybe, just maybe I'm not interested?" she asks defiantly.

The corner of her lip dances in an invisible smile. She's gorgeous, not in that conventional Hollywood beauty style or the cute next door girl type. She's a style all her own. Words wouldn't do her justice.

"I remember you being very interested in the limo," I remind her.

I didn't want to, but she poked me right in the ego. That's not playing fair.

"I was drunk," she pouts, like an offended child. "I just felt like kissing someone, anyone. Besides, I don't remember you being particularly interested. What changed your mind now?"

She sounds hurt. There's no mistaking the voice of a woman who believes she was wronged, that she was offended somehow. Obviously, me not accepting to kiss her when she thought I would didn't sit right with her.

"I don't kiss drunk girls," I explain something I thought was plain as daylight.

She raises her eyes to mine again. Her will is like a force field. First it was up, unbreakable, unyielding. Now, it seems that I found a crack in it.

"I like both parties to be sensible," I smile at the play of words. "Unless we're both drinking together, and we know what's gonna happen next."

I see that lingering frustration leaving her. Her body relaxes. Even her stare isn't as intense with defiance as before. I just want to wrap my arms around her and feel her wet warmth. Does she even know she's got that effect on men?

"Oh..." she musters. "Well... that's nice of you then, I guess."

I laugh. Then, unwilling and incapable of resisting her presence, I take a step closer to her. She doesn't pull away. I'm so close I feel her warm breath on my cheek, on the tips of my lips.

One of my hands is pressed flat against the low of her back, fingers splayed like a web. She can step away. She can push me away. But I know she doesn't want to.

"Have dinner with me, Grace," I whisper, my cock hard, still at a safe distance from her. If it even brushes against her skin, I won't be held accountable for my actions.

My hand tightens reflexively. Her body is driving me mad, hidden in that wide coat as if she's got something to hide. A body to kill for, to die for. Her gaze pierces through me, scorchingly intense.

My lips are dry. I want her tongue to wet them. But not yet.

Suddenly, she manages to fight me off. She lifts her gaze, her lips only a few inches away from mine. But, neither of us willing to make the first step.

"Just dinner?" she asks, a few loose strands of her glossy hair framing her beautiful face.

"Of course," I nod.

Was it a lie? I'm not sure myself. If it was, it wasn't a conscious lie.

"This isn't a date."

"No-one will call it that," I assure her, admiring the way she still wants to stick to her guns.

Besides, I'm not into dating. To much hassle. But, perhaps tonight will lead to something more, and I'm definitely willing to go through the hassle of one dinner for the promise of Grace's body.

"This will be me makings amends for those shirts I ruined," she reminds me.

"I actually didn't want to put a gun to your head to make you have one dinner with me," I smile. "But you do owe me for the shirts. A dinner, a mean."

"I'd rather pay for them," she pouts again.

"Trust me, you're better off enjoying a meal at my expense," I wink at her. Amazingly, she blushes a little, lowering her gaze, but the next moment, it is up again, as cheeky and rebellious as before.

She sighs. "Fine."

"Yes?" I ask. "My car is there."

I gesture across the street with my hand.

"Now?" she grimaces.

"It's dinner time, isn't it?"

"But I've just gotten off work," she starts.

"Which means you're hungry," I finish her thought, although not in the way she wanted it finished, I'm sure.

"I haven't even taken a shower."

I lean over, pressing my cheek against hers. She feels so warm. I inhale deeply, loudly. Then, I pull back equally quickly.

"You don't smell," I chuckle.

In fact, she's good enough to eat. But I keep this to myself.

"Why can't you do anything like a normal person?" She rolls her eyes at me, but she's not fooling me. She loves it. She's enjoying the game as much as I am. And, when it finally happens, we're going to fuck like hungry animals.

"Because normal things are boring. Don't tell me you like them?"

"They're easier to adjust to. Like, for example, why can't we just arrange this dinner for tomorrow night or something? Why does it have to be now?"

"Because I might get hit by a car tomorrow and fall into a deep coma," I give her one version of events from a parallel universe that might exist along with ours. "Then you'll be sorry you didn't have dinner with me right now."

"A coma, huh?" she shakes her head at me, sighing. "Fine. Let's do this. I wouldn't want you to fall into a coma."

I'm still laughing as we cross the street. I open the car door for her, and she gets in.

Not a date.

Her words echo in my mind. Hell no. If everything goes according to plan, then she'll get exactly what she wanted from the get-go.

Chapter 14

I don't even know where Rocco has brought me, but the moment I get out of his car, I see it. We're right in front of La Bella Cucina. It's the hottest Italian restaurant in town, and the waiting list is endless. You have to make a reservation weeks ahead, and even then it's not sure they will be able to accommodate you. Alisa and I tried arranging it once, but it was impossible.

Now, I'm left wondering if he planned this ahead and has a reservation, but maybe his date canceled, and now he thinks he'll take me instead. I immediately regret this thought, hoping that he's not such a pig.

"Mia dolce signorina," he tells me, interrupting my train of thought and offering me his hand. "Get ready to have an orgasm of taste."

I raise my eyebrow at him.

"Too much?" he asks innocently, with a smile that instantly dropped women's panties. Well, mine were still in a knot. No dropping here.

"A little," I frown. "But I am curious about this place."

"Best Italian food you'll ever have," he assures me.

When he sees that I won't accept his hand, he takes my hand and shoves it underneath his elbow, and we walk inside like that. Now even more so than before, I am aware of being a hot mess, not even having taken a shower and dressed like a secretary.

Two women pass us by. The one in the red, curve-hugging dress with a sway even Marilyn Monroe would die for, stares right at him, leaning over to her friend to whisper something. Silently, they chuckle to themselves, but her eyes never left him. She even turned around when they are at the door, in hopes that he would glance in her direction.

He did not.

Unconsciously, I dig my fingers into the soft skin of his inner elbow, and he turns to me puzzled.

"Sorry," I say, unaware of the reactions he was making me have. "Just a tick."

"OK," he smiles. Then, he turns to the hostess, yet another gorgeous woman who seems more fitted to be hanging at his hand. "Good evening."

"Oh, Mr. Barbati," she gushes, her voice deep and throaty, so sexy you'd think you just dialed a hot line by mistake. "Should we set up your usual table?"

"Yes," he nods nonchalantly. "And is Benedetto around?"

"Yes," she confirms, raising her hand and calling one of the free waiters, who immediately rushes over. She leans and whispers something in his ear, then a moment later, she is gone. "Your table will be ready in a moment, and Mr. D'Ovidio will join you in a moment."

"Thanks," he grins. "We'll just wait over there."

He points at the comfy looking sofas in the corner, which look like they were brought in from the Victorian exhibition at the local museum. I allow him to take me there, but before we can even get comfortable, I hear someone shouting Rocco's name.

"Eh, Rocco!"

I have to admit, his name sounds even hotter when someone with a real Italian accent pronounces it. We both turn around at the same time, and I see a man of about sixty, wearing a sharp auburn suit. The top button of his crisp, white shirt is undone, and when he gets closer to us, his cologne ricochets all around us.

"Benedetto," Rocco smiles, shaking his hand. "Come va?"

"Bene, bene," the man replies, his chiseled chin and jawline as straight as a knife. His skin is tanned, as if he just got back from the beach. "And who is this dove?"

I immediately blush under his gaze. This man is who Rocco will be in twenty years. Older. Worldly. Absolutely irresistible. Even his grey hair only adds to his charm. Like fine wine...

As if Rocco wasn't all those things already. Only minus the grey hair.

"This is my friend, Grace," Rocco introduces us.

"Very nice to meet you, Mr. D'Ovidio."

I offer him my hand, and his fingers graze mine, as he lowers his head and places a soft kiss on the upper part of my hand. Unused to such charms, I feel a little overwhelmed. Everything about this place and about these two men overwhelms me, but I try to focus on not making a fool of myself.

"Oh, no, cara," he tells me. "Benedetto. Ben, if you wish."

"I actually prefer your full name. It has more fire," I dare to comment, and the look on his face is priceless.

His eyes widen in disbelief. His gaze travels over to Rocco, then back at me.

"Oh, I like this one, Rocco. Where do you find them?"

Them. I'm not the only one. It was stupid to even assume I was or ever would be, but it still hit exactly the wrong place, dripping a little bit of salt on the wound.

"She works for me," Rocco explains.

"Ah, no woman as beautiful as you should ever work," Benedetto shakes his head.

There is something about him, something sophisticated and at the same time, soft.

"You are very kind to say that, but we live in the twenty-first century," I remind him.

"Ah, you feminists," he clicks his tongue in disapproval. "The only place where I want us to be equals is in bed. The rest, no."

Rocco laughs, although I don't find it as amusing as he does.

"Don't take it the wrong way," Rocco explains. "Now, what about our table?"

"It should be ready, I think," Benedetto turns around and raises his hand. The hostess nods. "It is ready. Let me take you there."

"No need, Benedetto," Rocco assures him.

"So, you alone could walk this beauty and show her off? Dimenticalo."

With those words, he takes me by the hand, and we start walking. I lean backward, and whisper to Rocco.

"What did he say?"

"He said, forget about it," he grinned, allowing Benedetto to guide us to our table.

We settle shortly at an oval shaped table, with a pristine white tablecloth. There is a small vase in the middle, with three blood red roses in it, in full bloom. The same waiter from before slides two fancy menus before us, with paper that has pearly sheen all over it.

"Some white wine? We've got a marvelous Domaine d'Auvenay Criots-Batard," he says it with a perfect French accent.

"Si," Rocco nods. "For dinner, surprise us."

"As always," Benedetto grins. "You won't be disappointed."

"I have yet to be," Rocco steals my glance.

Benedetto whispers something about the wine to the waiter, and he nods. Finally, a few moments later, we are alone, although the place is packed. I take a chance to look around. Everything inside feels like it belongs to a different era, or at least a different country. The chairs are covered in white cloth, with dainty lace at the edges. The floor is carpeted, smooth. Above us, in the middle of what seems to have once been used as a grand ballroom, I see the most monumental of chandeliers I've ever seen.

"This place feels like some old remnant from the Victorian era," I smile, lowering my gaze back at him, surprised to see that he hasn't taken his eyes off of me for a single moment.

"It is just like any other place," he tells me. "It is dependent on the people that inhabit it. Beautiful people make a beautiful place."

"What about deserted old chateaus and castles? Overgrown in weeds, and dilapidated. I find them absolutely breathtaking, but there are no people there to make them beautiful. How does your theory feel about that?" I ask him fiercely, teasing him to question his own theory about pretty people.

Of course, he would be interested in pretty people. But beauty is not everything. Not even when you looked that hot in graphite grey pants and just a simple dark green V-neck sweater.

It hits me then. This is not his work attire. The bastard has gone home and changed his clothes, not allowing me to do the same. Looking at him, I'm still wondering what exactly he wants. To jump straight into bed with me?

"In that case, I enforce the it's in the eye of the beholder adage," he replies. Leaning over to me, he adds. "By the way, you look..."

Messy? Tired? Annoyed? All of those could be used and he wouldn't be wrong.

"Good enough to eat," he chooses the one that wasn't even on my list.

"Really?" I chuckle. "You'll go with that one?"

"What?" he shrugs, pretending to be all shocked. "We're in a restaurant. It's a good joke."

"It's a decent joke," I correct him. "But you also look nice."

"Just nice?"

"Nice is... nice," I chuckle.

"Nice is when you have nothing else to say."

He's got me there. I do have a whole lot of things to say about him right now, but all of them would make me a little uncomfortable to say them to his face.

"Well, you look- "

"Gorgeous? Fabulous? Amazing? Utterly handsome?" he offers me some options which make us both laugh.

"Well, why ask when you already know the answer?" I wonder.

His brow arches. "I didn't think there was anything you liked about me. Not after the limo incident."

That limo incident will never go away, I think. His piercing blue stare is unbearable.

"So, do you come here often?" I spit out the first cliché that comes to mind. It doesn't matter what it is, as long as it gets us away from the limo incident.

"Yeah," he nods, leaning back in his chair to allow the waiter to pour us both some wine. "To mishaps."

"Really?" I wonder, and I can see the amusement on his face.

"If you didn't spill coffee on me, we wouldn't be here."

"If you had kissed me in the limo, we wouldn't be here," I remind him, but the moment I say it, I want to take it back. Of course, that's impossible.

"We could correct that mistake easily," he winks at me. "As I plan on doing. Now, let us drink to mishaps."

"Are you really supposed to be drinking when driving?" I pretend that I didn't hear about that kissing part.

He puts his glass down on the table and starts laughing. A few women around throw their seemingly casual glances at him, peppering him with flirtatious smiles. Jealousy stabs me in the stomach. I should have been more persistent and not let him take me out to dinner like this.

And yet, he looks only at me.

"I'm driving now, but in cases when I drink too much, I call for my driver," he explains. "But I don't plan on drinking more than a few sips, I assure you. Also -"

"Why if it isn't Rocco Barbati?"

I hear a girl's voice, and for some reason, she sounds familiar, as she walks up from somewhere behind me.

Chapter 15

Grace

When I turn around, I recognize her immediately. She is dressed less formally and more fitting for a night out. Still, her killer looks are undeniable. A part of me wants to run away to the bathroom and hide, but it's a little too late for that.

"Sonya," I decide to take over the conversation and steer it in the direction I want it to go.

Obviously, she's here for a reason, and I doubt it's to say hi to me. No way. She's looking at him like a black widow about to devour her mate and turn it into her prey. Then, it hits me. Could it be that something's going on between them? She sounds too chummy for someone who's just an employee.

"How nice to see you here," I smile at her, once she approached the table and stood right in the middle, so both Rocco and I could see her clearly.

"I had no idea you two knew each other," Sonya flashed her pearly whites at me.

"We don't," I rush to reply. "Not in a way other than boss and employee, that is."

Everything I say seems wrong. I'm so desperate to provide a plausible explanation for being here with him of all people, that I sound confused and apprehensive. And, I have no idea why. Not like I need to explain myself to anyone, least of all to someone who works in the same building I do.

Only, there's something about her gaze which is not allowing me to have my peace of mind. The way she approached us, swaying and waltzing over like she owned the place, rubbed me the wrong way. And that hand on his shoulder seems all too friendly.

"But this is a friendly dinner, isn't it?" Sonya squints at me, her eyes flaring up, daring me.

"Yes," he finally joins in, his voice refusing to admit exactly how he feels about it, and that makes me even more suspicious. "We were about to enjoy a nice friendly dinner, when you popped up."

Is that a raised eyebrow I see? But there is no annoyance on his part, or joy at seeing her.

"Oh, you," she chuckles, as if he just said the funniest thing in the world. "I remember when you took me here once."

That one punches me right in the belly, expelling all the air out of my lungs, but I manage to remain calm. So, that's why she's here. She's jealous. And she wants to make it known.

"I take a lot of my friends here," he replies casually, but I can tell that the unease at the table is rising.

She's not welcome here, but she remains. And we'd be the rude ones if we asked her to leave. Go figure.

"Well, we were a little more than just friends, weren't we Roc?"

The way she called him Roc seemed to rub him the wrong way. He swallows heavily, his fingers drumming nervously now against the table. Am I the third wheel here or is she? I wonder.

"It was really nice seeing you, Sonya," he says, without any intention of answering her question. "But, if you'll excuse us now, we're trying to enjoy each other's company."

With those words, he stares me down, and his face relaxes again. He's smiling, as if he magically wished her away. Poof! Just like that – and she's gone. I smile back at him, shocked at the way he dealt with her, but then again, she seemed to be asking for it, coming over in such an obvious, passive-aggressive way, demanding attention. She could have just waved, and everything would have been alright. Only, somehow, I know this isn't the last time we clash.

A veil of redness appears on her cheek, and suddenly, with those clenched teeth and pursed lips, she isn't pretty any longer. It's amazing what anger does to your face.

She suddenly slams her open palm against the table so hard, I wince and pull back. He doesn't even move. A wicked flare in her eyes stabs right through me, filling me up with uneasiness and even fear.

"Have a nice evening, you two," she grins, then turns around and leaves.

I take a deep, theatrical breath.

"And, here I was, thinking she was a nice person," I say, my eyes wide with shock and disbelief. "I actually met her on my first day and she seemed so nice, she even helped me in the elevator."

"She's a loose cannon," he shrugs. "Sorry about that."

"No, it's not your fault."

I don't know why I've said that. Of course, it's his fault. Whose else would it be? But I can't seem to say it out loud.

"It is true that I brought her here once," he continues. "And, we also did have a one-night stand."

I feel another stab of jealousy, right below the belt. A low blow. Well, of course they had a one-night stand. That was pretty obvious.

"You..." I shake my head at him, grabbing my glass of wine again, more as a distraction than out of thirst. "You didn't need to share that. Such things are private."

"To be quite honest, I don't kiss and tell," he confides, and for some reason, I believe him. He really doesn't seem like the boyish type to be bragging about all the tail he's had. That's good. "But, as you can see, sometimes it's out of my hands."

"Yeah," I snort.

I actually thought this would be a fun night, but between him accosting me in front of my building and Sonya turning out to be a total loon, I've realized that it's probably for the best to quickly eat my food and head on home, before something even crazier happens.

"I just didn't want there to be any secrets or lies between us," he suddenly tells me, leaning over the table, so that now his finger is drawing circles on the white tablecloth.

"Why?" I ask, truly curious.

We're not friends. I doubt that's what he wants us to be.

"Because I'm intrigued by you."

"I'm not looking to date," I immediately tell him.

Up to a certain point, it's the truth. I barely have enough time for myself, let alone for someone else. But I haven't excluded the possibility of having occasional fun without any exaggerated expectations.

"Great," he chuckles, with a wicked gleam in his eye. "Neither am I."

"Good, we're in agreement on that one," I smile. "I haven't got any left-over time to squeeze in anything that might take a toll on my personal life."

"Couldn't have said it better myself," he grins. "But I do like fun."

"Fun as in sex?"

"Exactly. Do we agree on that one?"

"Um, sure," I nod, caught a little off guard. I wasn't expecting this to be a conversation where I would need to state my preference for sex. "I like sex."

"Then have it with me," he leans over and says it so seriously that I absolutely cannot take him seriously, so I burst out into laughter.

"Does that approach ever work?" I wonder, eyeing him carefully, my mouth twitching in hidden amusement.

"What did I say about kissing and telling?" he reminds me.

"OK, OK," I chuckle, that wine glass still in my hand. This time, I actually bring it to my lips. "What did you say before we were so rudely interrupted? To mishaps?"

He smiles, and it's like someone turned on a lightbulb in pitch dark. Dazzling and enigmatic. If I didn't know it before, I know it now. I doubt I'll be able to keep pushing him away much longer.

Why was I doing it in the first place? Was it still out of some misplaced sense of pride that he didn't want it when I wanted it? Alisa would call it not just silly, but downright ridiculous. And, I have to admit, I somehow agreed.

"To mishaps," he raises his glass to clink with mine, and the chaos of emotions takes me by storm.

Chapter 16

Rocco

I tell the driver to drop us off in front of her building. Turns out that I couldn't resist having another glass of wine with her. Or, two. Or, three. And, here we are again, in my car. It feels like déjà vu. Maybe I won't fuck it up this time.

"Thanks for a lovely dinner," she says, clutching at her bag underneath her left arm.

Her hair became a little undone. Now it's more of a messy bun, with that I just got out of bed look. That's definitely a look that suits her. In my bed, or in hers. I'm not partial to beds. Floors have worked just fine in the past.

"I'm glad you enjoyed it," I reply.

She's smirking. She looks like she wants to tell me something. This is not a night to talk. It's a night to act.

"I guess that makes us even," she adds, sounding a little sad.

"Of course not," I shake my head at her.

"What?" she gasps.

Her red cheeks look like apples. You just want to take a bite of her. You want to tell her everything she wants to hear, because you want to see her happy. You want her to give herself to you. Only... where will that lead?

"You ruined two of my most expensive shirts," I lie. Luckily, she doesn't know that. "This was only one dinner."

"But you said dinner would make us even."

"Did I?" I lean back, tilting my head.

Fucking Hell. How does old Hoffman look at her all day long without wanting to ravish her? She seems so sweetly innocent, but you know that when you scratch beneath the surface, you'll be surprised by what you find there.

That's exactly what I'm waiting – for her to let me scratch underneath her surface and see what wonders she is hiding. Then, we'll probably both get bored of this game and that'll be that.

I can only hope that she won't be like Sonya. Great lay. Lousy aftermath. I've always been pretty clear about these things. I don't date. I don't do relationships. I haven't got the time or the will or the desire to deal with any of that drama. She knew what she was getting into when she accepted my invitation to dinner. It's a one-way ticket for the lucky ones. Once the ride is over, that's that. Game over. I thought we were clear on that.

It seemed she wasn't. She was calling me all day long. She would come up to my office, unannounced. I even had to instruct my own secretary to keep her out, at the threat of losing her own job.

Finally, it worked. At least, I thought it did, and tonight made me less convinced.

"Two shirts mean twice," I tell her.

"Twice what?"

Leaving her without a reply, I lean in and I kiss her. Just like that. I don't know if she saw it coming or not, but she doesn't pull back. I can taste the sweet wine still on her lips. She tastes like the summer, warm and delicious, and you just want more and more.

It becomes too much to bear, all this explosive, pent up energy and the emotions she's been causing. She moans slightly, barely audibly, but I hear it. My cock springs up, viciously, aching for release.

With my lips still pressed against hers, I grab her by the hair, her bun now completely loose, with curls falling out to frame her flushed face. Unexpectedly, she takes my tongue and starts sucking on it. I groan, adjusting the length of my cock, which now threatened to tear my pants. It's a kiss of passion, of desperate need, a kiss which if left untended, wouldn't have an end.

Completely overwhelmed with desire, I wrench away, because if I keep going, I won't be able to stop myself. She's breathing heavily, her lips parted, wet with desire.

"Does this make us even?" she asks playfully, staring me right in the eyes.

"Not even close," I tell her. "I said twice."

"But you didn't explain."

"Two dinners. Two places. Not necessarily us eating."

I raise my eyebrow and she immediately gets the hint.

"Ooooh," she elongates it. She lifts her finger and points behind her, in the direction of the building. "I think I know exactly what you mean."

"That makes me very glad," I grin.

She leans over to me again. I can still smell the lingering fragrance of her perfume which she put on this morning. Now, it has soaked up into her skin. It is the smell of her, only sweetened up.

She is so close, our lips are almost touching. I'm titillated to see whether she'll make the first move this time.

Surprisingly or not, she does. She traces a line on my face with her finger, then down to my ear, tickling my earlobe. I can barely control myself. I aim at her, lips open, about to devour her with my second kiss, but she immediately pulls back.

"It's a workday tomorrow, but I see you don't care about that," she teases.

"You forget I'm the boss. I can come whenever I want, then just stay longer, or even not come at all."

"Yes, that's you," she nods. "But not me."

Her body straightens itself, like a flower after rain. She dusts off her skirt, then stares right at me, her hand already on the door, ready to push it open any moment.

"Thanks again for the dinner. Good night, Rocco."

With those words, she leaves my car, and leaves me throbbing in more ways than one. I grin as I watch her leave, her stride confident and content.

Shit. I should really focus more on work and less on her.

Easier said than done.

Chapter 17

Grace

It's a busy morning at work, and I barely have any time for my coffee. Mr. Hoffman kept me occupied in his office, but when he offered to have lunch together, I shook my head. Not because I found it indecent or strange, because I didn't, but simply because I'd already brought a ready-made lunch in the form of Caesar's salad, just in case I didn't get the chance to leave my desk again.

This time I did have enough time, but I felt a little lazy. I nestled into my cozy chair and opened the yellow lunchbox which Alisa packed for me. Sometimes, I think she pampers me too much, but that's what you get when you have awesome best friends. They take good care of you and your stomach.

I glance over at my coffee mug. About three hours ago, it smelled divine. Someone had ordered for the set-up of a new coffee machine, and the beverage it makes is absolutely divine. Only, this morning I did not get a chance to enjoy it while it was hot, and now that it's cold, it serves little to no purpose.

So, instead, I focus on the salad. As always, Alisa's skills in the kitchen are amazing. She always says it's just an amateurish skill, but it's enough to make anyone's mouth water.

When I'm about half done with my salad, a guy walks over to my desk, carrying a cardboard box in his hands.

"Are you Grace Hensley?" he asks.

From his uniform, I could tell he's a delivery man of sorts, although I can't tell who he works for.

"I have a package for you," he tells me, while I'm still trying to remember if maybe Alisa or I ordered something online, and then just forgot about it. It sounds doubtful, but so many things have happened in the last two weeks that I wouldn't put it past myself.

He puts the box on my desk, then extracts a pad and offers it to me to sign.

"Do I need to pay anything?" I wonder, hesitating to accept the pen.

"No, it's all been paid for," he informs me, the pen still in his hand.

I sigh, accepting it, then scribbling my signature quickly. He nods quickly, wishes m a good day, and disappears, leaving me in the usual clamor of the big office.

I stare at the box, almost as if it were a bomb and the last thing I should do is touch it. But curiosity gets the best of me. Maybe I really did order something online, and now it'll be a surprise. That's how you surprise yourself, you see. Genius.

I take a small pair of scissors and cut along the line of the dark brown scotch tape. My fingers tingle with anticipation as I open the upper cover. There is cushioning tissue paper inside, and it's the first thing I see.

Then, I see it. There's a box inside this box. It's smaller, expensive looking, ruby red with a satin white ribbon wrapped around it, tied in a bow. I untie it and open the box. The rich fragrance of chocolate spreads all around me. There is a white chocolate one. Dark chocolate. Milk chocolate with coffee? I lower my head to intake the smell, and it's amazing. White chocolate with raspberries drizzled all over it. Tiny, bite sized pieces nestled in little cases, twelve in total.

By the chocolates, cozied up inside the cushioning paper, there is a card. Excited, I reach for it, but I could guess who it was from. He's trying to win an uncharted territory and I must admit, he's doing a fine job of it.

There isn't much written on the card. Just a Call me and a number. Not even a name. The first letter of a name. Nothing.

I raise my eyebrow thinking how bold he is. How undaunting. So, he's thinking about me. Is that a good thing? At this point, I honestly don't know. In the beginning, I somehow managed to convince myself that sleeping with the boss of all bosses wouldn't be such a big deal. Right now, I'm not so sure.

However, one thing's for sure. The knowledge that he's been thinking about me long and hard enough to send me a box of assorted chocolates makes me feel all giddy. Whatever happens, perhaps I should just enjoy the moment and go with the flow, stop overanalyzing stuff.

I was already in trouble when it came to Rocco Barbati. In deep, deep trouble. Worst of all? I started it.

I take the first delectable bite of the white chocolate with raspberry, and I let it melt in my mouth. It feels like a taste of heaven. My hand flies over to the phone, and a moment later, I would have called him. But I managed to resist the urge.

Am I into him? Definitely.

Is he into me? Hmm... sure seems so.

Maybe some casual and animalistic sex without any strings attached would be just the right thing here. No expectations. No responsibility towards each other. Just fun.

So, instead of him, I dial Alisa, and tell her all about the present which just arrived.

"Giiiiirl!" she squeals on the other end of the line. "He so wants to get in your panties."

"You know what?" I throw a quick glance around, just to make sure that there's no-one around who might overhear my conversation. "I actually might let him do it."

She chuckles. "That's my girl! Maybe it even turns into something serious. Just imagine, you and- "

"I don't think so," I shake my head immediately at the thought.

I doubt I'd be able to control my jealousy. Wherever he goes, women are all over him. I know it's just a matter of trust, but still. I didn't have many boyfriends, but I did have one pretty boy. Downside? Every woman wanted to fuck him, and he eventually fell under that spell, totally forgetting about me. I wish it were so easy for me to forget being betrayed like that. So, no. I don't think so.

"Rocco Barbati is not the kind of guy you'd expect to sail off into the sunset with," I explain. "He's the kind for an explosive one-night stand, and that's exactly what I plan on using him for."

"Well, OK then. You seem to know what you're doing."

"Actually, no," I laugh. "I have absolutely no idea what I'm doing. But that's the fun, right?"

"Sure thing," she joins in the laughter. "Oh, it's a good thing you called."

"It is?"

"Yeah, I've been meaning to text you, but I haven't gotten around to it yet. I'll be out for the night, so you're not worried when you come home tonight."

"Thanks for the heads up. Who's the lucky winner?"

"Oh, just some guy I picked up on Tinder."

"Oh, watch out for those. They can be crazy," I frown. "Turn on your location, so I know where you are."

"Always do," she reminds me. "What'll you do tonight?"

"Well, seeing I have the apartment so rarely all to myself... I'll just have a nice, long bubble bath, enjoy a glass of wine and probably doze off before I even finish the first chapter of this new book I've started."

"Sounds like an old grandma's idea of a good night," she chuckles.

"Oh, ha-ha," I pretend to be offended.

"Maybe you could call Mr. Italian over?"

"No way."

"Why not?"

"Let him wait a little."

"Oh, that's the game you're playing?" she asks me, and I nod like an old sage who knows exactly what he is doing. I myself don't, but it feels good to pretend otherwise. "Seems you need no more advice from anyone."

"Hardly, but I'll take the compliment," I chuckle. "I have to finish my lunch and go back to work. Enjoy yourself tonight."

"You, too, Agatha," she teases. "Bye!"

I'm still smiling when I hang up the phone. I leave the box of chocolates right on the desk, and go back to my lunch, then to my work. Every time my glance wanders over to it, something gurgles in my stomach. And it's not the salad. It's that knot that keeps reminding me how much I want to call him and invite him over. But I still don't.

I finish my work for the afternoon and head on home. It's pleasantly empty. Not that I mind Alisa being there. I love her presence. I love the fact that I get to have my best friend as a roommate as well. But, sometimes, all you want is to be alone with your own thoughts.

I start the water, pouring a little bit of bath salts and some oil, which immediately starts to create lovely foam. The aroma of cinnamon and orange is in the air, and I inhale deeply, relishing it. A few candles are scattered about the bathroom, in safe places, so that they wouldn't start a fire, even accidentally.

I peel off my clothes, one layer at a time, just letting them drop down to the ground in disarray. One by one, my blouse, my skirt, my stockings, my bra and undies end up on the floor. Released from the shackles of clothes, I walk over to the bathtub, which is already half filled with water and the other half has overflowing bubbles. I stop the water, ready to dive in.

The moment my toe touches the surface of the now still water, I hear the doorbell.

"What the..." I speak out loud, shocked that I'm actually hearing it.

I frown. It couldn't be Mr. Weasley from the fifth floor, who comes every month for donations to the local dog pound. He already came this month. Besides, he never comes this late, and on a workday. It has to be someone else. But, who?

At first, I don't want to find out. I wait to see if they'll ring the bell again. If they don't, great. I'll just slide into my bathtub and pretend like this never happened.

Only, I can't. The second time the bell rings, it's much more persistent. Whoever is on the other side of the door, really wants to talk to either me or Alisa.

Cursing underneath my breath, I grab my bathrobe from the hanger in the bathroom and tighten the belt. I make sure to close the upper part as much as I can. I stomp over to the door, and the third attack of the bell hits me.

"Hold your horses," I growl from inside, unlocking the door then unlatching it. "I actually heard the bell the first time, no need to be so..."

But, the moment I open the door, I see him. Only him. And the rest of the world just fades away.

Chapter 18

Grace

"Rocco..."

The moment I see him, I feel like someone threw me right in the middle of a conversation where I not only didn't know everyone involved, but I also had no idea what they were talking about in the first place. For a few moments, I can't do or say anything. I just stare at him in stunned silence.

He looks like he just got off work. Strangely enough, it's actually me who is undressing him with my eyes, instead of it being the other way around.

"What are you doing here?" I gasp, glancing behind him down the hallway, just to make sure that no one was walking by.

"Did you get my chocolates?" he says instead of replying, walking over to me, but making sure to remain on the outer side of the doorway.

I immediately think of a vampire. He can't come into a house, unless he has been invited first. The thought makes me smile. If anyone would be doing any sucking around me or on me, I'd sure love it to be him.

But I'm trying not to show him how excited I am to see him here.

"I did, thank you," I nod. "They were delicious."

It's at that moment that he rakes me with his eyes, lingering on the bare skin of my neck. My bathrobe has separated only enough for me to still remain politely covered, but that V-neck could still conceal promises.

"Is that why you came?" I wonder.

"No," he shakes his head at me. "May I come in?"

"Sure," I step to the side to let him in, then the moment he does so, I lock the door behind him. "Is anything wrong?"

It's a silly question, really. But I don't know what else to ask. His presence is making me feel excited and nervous at the same time, even more so because he's here, in my apartment.

"Yes, something is very wrong," he tells me gravely, approaching me.

At this point, I'm trying to figure out if maybe I made a terrible mistake at work, and Mr. Hoffman called Rocco, who, not seeing any other way of handling it, had to come here to talk to me.

"Did I do something wrong?" I ask, now even more worried.

"It's not what you did," he shakes his head at me, his eyes glaring. "It's what you didn't do."

I try to remember a missed deadline or some tasks I had which I didn't do. Nothing comes to mind.

"You didn't call me, even though my card specifically said to do so."

"What..." I look at his breathtaking face all incredulous, wondering if I heard it right. Unable to resist, I chuckle out loud. "Was there some kind of a deadline?"

"No, just an urge," he explains, now already invading my personal space.

We're once again as close as we were in his car, and I know what's going to happen. The very thought makes me hot, needy for those lips to kiss mine again.

"An urge I can't control..." There is a raw, animalistic growl to his voice which sends shivers down my spine.

Having him here, in front of me is too much. His masculine scent is all over me, penetrating my every pore, just like an image of his has penetrated my every thought. I know now that, from the moment I saw him, I've been falling down a rabbit hole, not even seeing the bottom. And I didn't care one bit.

When he kisses me that second time, all my inhibitions come undone.

"Are you alone?" he mumbles against my lips.

"Yes..." I moan, completely melting into him, allowing his arms to envelop me on both sides and pull me closer to him. "But- "

I try to protest, but he doesn't let me. His lips fall right over mine, wet and lush. His tongue curiously explores, and the naughty part of me wonders what it would feel like to have him do that on another body part of mine.

Completely overwhelmed, I dig my fingers into his hair, tugging at it gently. He groans with pleasure. Together, we stumble back towards the sofa in the living room, on the way there almost bumping over a small table in the corner.

We sit together on the sofa, and his hand is fumbling with the rope to my robe, which gives way easily. I gasp, but his lips stifle my voice.

"Rocco..." His name is so sensual, I could keep saying it over and over again.

"Gorgeous Grace," he whispers, as his hand slides inside my robe, and his fingers find my perky nipples. "You're driving me crazy..."

I feel him teasing the tip of my breast, heat arising from somewhere deep inside of me. There is a storm brewing inside both of us. It has been brewing for such a long time that I doubt either of us will be able to stop ourselves. Insane and completely inexplicable, I want to give it all up to him. One night of wild passion.

He breathes heavily into my ear, as one of his hands pushes its way between my legs. I feel so hot, I'm bordering on feverish. His skilled fingers find my velvet underground easily. Every part of my body is aching to the touch, unbearably sensitive to what he's doing to me. I'm already wet for him, ready for whatever he wants.

"You feel so tender to the touch," he murmurs. "So soft... so wet..."

Slowly, while still kissing me fervently, he slides a finger inside of me. He's leaning over me, but then he slides down to the floor. When I open my eyes and look at him, he's on his knees. Rocco Barbati is on his knees for me.

A tidal wave of warmth washes over me, and I close my eyes, allowing the sensation to erase any other notion apart from the sight of Rocco's face and the delicate touch of his fingers. He pulls it out slowly, then slides two fingers back inside, slowly stretching me as he goes.

I bite my lower lip, my back arching to accommodate him. I feel greedy, selfish. I want all that he has to give, and I want it now. But he's keeping it painfully slow, teasing me.

Once again, he pulls out, then slides two fingers back in. I moan more loudly this time, delight searing through my skin, burning through any leftover defenses of logic I had up to this point. His thumb circles my swollen clit, rubbing it gently. I dig my fingers into the cushions next to me, pushing myself onto his fingers for more depth.

When I open my eyes, I see his smug grin. He's happy with himself, that he's got me so helplessly responsive to him, writhing with pleasure at the touch of his hands. Fire explodes inside of me, and I know I'm close. Feeling it, too, he slows his rhythm, taking me back to the beginning and down the same road again, only this time, I can't take it anymore. My thighs are shaking, my entire body is trembling.

"Is it good?" he asks, breathing heavily, as if he himself were on the verge, too.

"God, yes…"

"I want it to feel good for you, Grace," he continues, his stroking fingers driving me crazier and crazier. "I want to feel you cum all over my fingers, my mouth and my cock. I want you to think about my cum inside of you, dripping down your thighs. I want you to be fully aware of the fact that you will do whatever I tell you to do, and you will do it gladly, because you know how it will make you feel, like the dirty girl that you are."

"Oh, God, yes…"

His voice is in my ears, and there is a distant ringing, a pent-up tension which begs to be released. Something is still holding me back, making me walk that fine line, looking into the abyss, but not ready to plunge downward. Not yet.

His rhythm is steady, he seems to be in rush, while I'm falling apart in his arms. I moan, digging my white-knuckled fingers even more deeply into the pillows, as his other hand rests on my stomach open-palmed. The heat is unbearable.

"Now, Grace..." he demands, and if anyone else said it, I'd just shake it off as some odd stupidity.

But not this time. Not with him. His words push me over the brink of an orgasm, and I keep falling down that same rabbit hole. I grind against his hand still, unable to take my eyes off his. There is a victorious smile on his lips, silent and deadly.

There is a loud waterfall in my ears, and I can't hear what he's saying. I guess I don't really need to. Still sensitive and bristled with pleasure, my lungs welcome the deep inhale of air. My eyes are closed. I'm relishing the moment.

All of a sudden, he takes one of my legs and rests it on his back. Then, a different tidal wave of hotness lights that fire all over again.

"Oh, Rocco..." I call out his name. "I need you... I need to feel you inside of me..."

I don't even know if he can hear me. Ecstasy boils up just beneath the surface of my skin as his tongue plays with my clit, licking it, teasing it, fluttering over it. Everything inside of me is throbbing with desperate need, and I never thought I'd be so close to a second orgasm right after the first one.

He doesn't even need to work hard for it this time. His finger joins in, sliding into my velvet wetness, while his tongue flicks over my clit frantically. My entire body tenses, my fingers digging into his hair, gripping at it as if my life depended on it.

Just a few seconds later, I climax again, imploding, coming completely undone. This time, he is merciful. He lets me be. Feeling like I don't have a single bone in my body, but rather being just a sack of skin, I breathe slowly, desperate for air.

He sits by my side, cupping my chin with his hand, then turning me to face him. Gently, he plants a kiss on my slightly sweaty forehead. My eyelids are heavy. I just want to close them and soak in the smell of him.

"Get some rest," he finally says, walking over to the door, but stopping once he grabbed the doorknob.

He turns to me, that look of triumph and smugness still on his face. Has he changed his mind about something?

"No fucking this time," he tells me, impishly. "You didn't call when I told you to, so leaving you like this, aching for more, is your punishment. Good night, Grace."

He unlocks the door and lets himself out.

Punishment? This, to him, is punishment? I chuckle out loud, my clit still throbbing in rhythm with his fingers. The pulsation is slowly dying down, but he's right. He's left me not satisfied, but exactly the opposite - desperate for more.

Chapter 19

Rocco

It's hard to focus on work this morning. Damn hard. I keep thinking about the previous night. How she smelled. How she moaned. How she called my name. I was a moment away from fucking her raw, right then and there. It took all my conscious effort to keep away from her. And punish her, in a way.

The game we've been playing is turning out to be the most interesting hunt I've had in years. Women lost the need to seduce. They point their fingers and that's that. There's such a lack of effort to fuck on both parts, and it was also a part of why I retreated. Not to mention that a family tragedy doesn't leave you in any mood for sex.

I sigh, leaning back in my chair. This office used to belong to my dad. I've been meaning to change it. The leather seems somehow outdated. The dark, oak shelves are bulky and awkward. The vibe seems off somehow to anyone who comes in. I've had more than one person comment on it.

Only, the more time passes, the less I'm inclined to do so. It's a trove of memories. A safe place. The only safe place in this entire building, maybe in this entire city. This and my home. I can lock up my home, and not see anyone. But I can't lock up my office. That wouldn't work.

I'm still lost in thought when my office door suddenly burst open. Sonya comes barging in, like she owns the place, and Veronica, my secretary, rushes after her, frantic and beside herself.

"Mr. Barbati, I'm so sorry... I kept telling her you were not to be disturbed, but she pushed me to the side and went right in. Should I call security?"

I see the look Sonya has. Come on. I dare you.

"It's fine, Veronica," I raise my hand, sighing and realizing that this day started off completely off the grid, but it seems it'll just keep getting worse. "No need to call security. Miss. Dawkins will state her business here, and then she will leave calmly, aren't you Miss. Dawkins?" I turn to her, trying to keep the peace.

"Of course," she raises her hands in a mock gesture of surrender.

Veronica doesn't seem convinced. She watches me from behind her thick-rimmed glasses, a wiry woman whom you'd always want on your side in any fight. I nod again, to assure her it's really fine.

"What'd on the agenda next?" I ask her quickly.

"You have a meeting with Mr. Freeman at 10," she informs me.

"Got it, thank you, Veronica."

She nods a little nervously, still unwilling to leave me alone with this woman, who has barged into my office more than anyone else. But that was months ago, and eventually, things have calmed down... or, so I thought.

"So, what do you want?" I move straight to the point, in no mood for idle chit chat, especially not with her.

Also, if I'm late for my meeting with George, he might go to someone else. I can't allow that. Not with the size of his project.

"Is that any way to talk to an old friend?" she purrs across the table, resting on her hands so low that I can see down her neckline. It's not where I want to look, so I keep my eyes on the same level as hers. The last thing I want to do is add more fuel to the fire by glancing at her cleavage.

"That's a good one," I chuckle, raking my fingers through my hair. She always makes me want a cigarette. It's the nerves. "You know we're not friends. We're nothing. Colleagues, but even that's a stretch."

"Well, that's not nice," she pouts, pretending to be offended.

"Nice or not, it is what it is," I've already grown tired of this, and I'm not even slightly amused. "So, you wanna tell me why you're here or do you really want me to call security?"

I'm bluffing. She knows it. Her father is one of our clients, bringing in heaps of money with every new project. I know that. She knows that.

Her working here is a favor to her father, who wants to teach her how to value money. As if.

Her nostrils flare at the insinuation, but I see no fear in those eyes, framed by dark eyeliner and fake eyelashes. Despite that fakeness, she's a beautiful woman. That's on first glance. On second glance, you realize she's a bit of a wacko. And I don't want to judge. Some people are into that. Not me though.

"Call them," she tests me.

"Honestly, I'm trying to avoid a scene," I try to stay calm. It's hard, but still doable. "And you've heard Victoria. I have a meeting in half an hour. Just tell me why you're back here again."

There's little point in asking, because we both know why. She's seen me with Grace, and she probably doesn't like it. I've heard that she still hopes that we'd be together or some stupid shit like that, even though I never gave any false promises. Never. I have a rule against it.

"If you want to date someone from around here, why don't you make it me?" she asks seductively, but it's not working on me. "I was here first."

She winks at me and lowers her breast to my gaze even more. No reaction. Not even a memory.

"If you're referring to Grace Hensley, we're not dating."

"You had dinner."

"So? Dinner isn't necessarily a date."

"With you, it's a prelude to something," she smiles slyly. "I remember how you took me to- "

"Listen," I interrupt her, getting up. "I'm trying to be nice here, but I'm really not in the mood to take a trip down memory lane with you. I was very clear with you."

"I was hoping I could make you change your mind," she says temptingly, walking around the desk and walking over to me.

She puts the tips of her fingers on my chest, then tiptoes down to my stomach. When she tries to go lower, I grab her by the wrist to stop her.

"Stop," I shake my head. "Don't."

"I remember it being the other way around," she laughs.

From the looks of it, this could go on for hours. She didn't come here to achieve a specific goal. She just came to annoy me, knowing she's got no chance.

"Sonya... please," I say as nicely as I can.

There is no point arguing with her or threatening her. Hell, most of the time not even being nice works. But I don't know what else to do. If she doesn't leave my office right now, I'll leave it myself. That's my last resort. Luckily, she agrees.

"OK," she nods, yanking her hand away from my grip. "But only because you said please."

I nod, sighing with relief.

"But don't think this is over," she throws me a backward glance before she leaves my office.

This time, she doesn't even slam the door behind her. I don't take her last comment very seriously. If she starts to become a problem, she'll go. It's as simple as that.

I sit down at my desk again. Grace is still in the back of my mind, but I realize that I have a shitload of work to do, and it won't do itself.

Chapter 20

Grace

When I return home from work that day, the moment I enter my apartment, I immediately remember the previous day. The image of that sofa is now forever changed in my mind. I'm honestly not even sure I mind.

"Hey, girl!" Alisa greets me from the kitchen. "You're just in time. I'm making some spaghetti bolognaise."

"Nice," I nod, letting my bag slide down from my shoulder and right onto the floor.

"You OK?" she eyes me from the kitchen, with a wooden spoon in her hand.

"Just a little tired," I explain. "Long day."

"Oh, and I thought it's because you couldn't sleep last night after what happened," she chuckles.

I walk over to the kitchen and sit at the table, so that now I'm looking straight at her, dancing around the stove as if she were born to hold that wooden spoon.

"Yes, I couldn't sleep," I confirm with a similarly amused chuckle. "And, yes, it has been a long day."

"OK then," she nods. "Did you see him today?"

"No," I shake my head.

"Did you want to?"

Her question catches me off guard.

"Honestly, I'm not sure. I probably wouldn't know what to expect or how to act."

"Well, you said you don't expect anything, right?"

"Yes, that would have been the case if we had slept together properly," I pout, enjoying the fragrant aroma which permeated the air. My stomach instantly reminds me that lunch was a long time ago.

"Properly?" she laughs, stirring the sauce a little before setting it on the table.

"You know what I mean," I'm still pouting. "That was just... teasing. Not fair. Now I want it even more."

"Seems like he knows the game well," she shrugs helplessly.

"He should," I nod. "He's probably been playing it longer than you and I put together."

"Is he that old?" she frowns.

"No, that's not what I meant," I laugh. "You know I don't have daddy issues. I meant he's got experience."

"Oh," she nods, and at that moment I hear the ping sound of my phone from my bag.

"I'm so lazy to get up now," I whine.

"Then, don't," she offers a pretty solid reply.

"Maybe it's work."

"You're off work now. Come on, you're not a slave."

"You're right," I smile.

But, at the same time, I get up and head over to my bag, getting my phone out. I slowly walk back into the kitchen, and she immediately notices my strangely serious face.

"See, I told you not to check the message," she scolds me. "What do they want now?"

I lift my head from the phone to look at her. My eyebrow is raised. I'm confused. Shocked a little, too. Curious. But, mostly shocked. This has never happened to me before.

"It's not work," I say.

It is then she realizes something's off.

"Who is it?"

She puts down the spoon and switches off the boiling spaghetti. I don't reply immediately. Instead, I read the message again. Then, once more for good measure, just to make sure I read it right.

"Come on, girl, you're freaking me out now," she urges, walking over to me and placing her hand on my shoulder.

"I just got an email from someone," I start.

"Who?"

"I don't know."

"What do they want?"

"They want me to, I quote, stay away from him."

She frowns. "From whom?"

"Rocco, probably," I shrug. "I don't see who else it could be."

"Just that? Nothing else?"

"Yes, just that."

"Any idea who it could be?"

"No... wait..." I suddenly remember Sonya at the restaurant. Alisa's curiosity is immediately piqued, and she leans over to me, as if we were in on a conspiracy and she needs new info now. "There's this girl at work- "

"Isn't there always?" Alisa laughs. "Sorry, go on."

"Well, she saw us at La Bella Cucina, walked over and... well, turns out they slept together in the past, and obviously, she doesn't like the idea that it's all in the past."

"She told you this?"

"She mentioned it, then he confirmed when she left. I didn't even ask, he just said it, because he didn't want there to be any lies between us."

"Wow, Mr. Barbati, those are some serious points you picked there," she whistles in admiration, which immediately makes me chuckle. "Like I said, his game is solid."

"His is, but what about this woman?" I ask, in predicament.

"Honestly, I wouldn't make it into a big deal just yet."

"You wouldn't?"

"No," she tells me, then gives a dismissive wave of her hand. "She didn't say anything specific, nothing that should scare you. Maybe she just felt angry and sent this email in a fit of rage, but she'll forget all about it by tomorrow morning, and she'll even feel silly. So, no. I'd leave it like this for now. But, if it happens again, then that's a different matter."

"Maybe you're right," I press my hands to my cheeks, with my elbows on the table. "It's probably nothing. Just female ego."

"Yeah," Alisa confirms. "Now, let's dig in before the spaghetti cools down."

She proceeds to pour me some and I do as she instructs. The food is delicious, and as always, Alisa makes it so easy to forget about any problems you might have, because she is so fun to be around with. She always has amusing stories from work, such as the one about a dog with an attack of diarrhea running through her office.

Only, this time, I can't forget about this email. Sure, it seems harmless enough.

But is it really?

Chapter 21

Grace

"Hey, Grace?" I hear Mr. Hoffman's voice over the phone. "Could you come to my office for a moment?"

"I'll be right there," I reply, hanging up and heading over there.

It's been day two since that fateful evening, and I haven't heard from Rocco. I guess, we're not dating, so I shouldn't be expecting anything from him. Only, I thought there was so much fire between us, and I was hoping that he'd be equally tempted for round two. But my pride wouldn't allow me to make the first move.

I knock on my boss' office and enter when called.

"Grace," he smiles upon seeing me.

He's dressed more casually today, with just a blue sweater and a dark pair of pants. He even looks a bit younger like this.

"Mr. Hoffman," I smile back.

"You've been a great help with the Collins account," he says eyeing me across the table. "I really appreciate it."

"That's what I'm here for," I nod pleasantly.

Now that the Collins project was finished, hopefully it'll be a little less hectic around here.

"What I also wanted to ask you is if you're free tonight."

The insinuation is obvious. But I'm trying to give him the benefit of the doubt.

"Um, yes, but why?" I sound suspicious, maybe even overly so.

"Well, you see," he smiles broadly, as he leans back into his chair contentedly. "I've been home more evenings these past few weeks since you started working, and my wife has been very happy with that, and she suggested for the three of us to go out somewhere for dinner. Nothing fancy, she just wants to express her gratitude for having me home in time to actually spend some quality time together with the family."

"Oh," I smile back, a little ashamed that I jumped to conclusions so easily. Hopefully, this will be a lesson learned. "That's very kind of both of you, but there's no need to thank me for anything. Like I said, I'm only doing my job, which I'm paid for."

By the time I say it, it sounds a little haughty.

"Would you consider doing it as a favor to a friend then?" he asks kindly.

"Of course," I nod immediately.

Why not? It's just a dinner, and I don't want to sound ungrateful or rude.

"When were you thinking of arranging this?"

"Well, we usually have no plan in the evenings, so we are pretty flexible."

"What about your daughter?" I wonder, remembering the birthday a while back.

"My wife's sister lives just a few blocks down, and her kids are all grown up. That's what you get when you start early, eh? So, she always jumps in whenever we need her."

"That's nice," I smile. "Well, then we could do it tomorrow maybe?"

"Perfect," he assures me. "I'll let my wife know."

"What's your wife's name?"

"Helen," he replies.

"Well, Mr. Hoffman, I'd love to have dinner with you and Helen," I say a little ceremoniously, although this does seem a bit odd.

It's probably just me, overthinking things again. Why wouldn't someone be a nice person, wanting to thank someone?

"It's a date then," he chuckles.

"Yeah," I smile at his joke. "Is there anything else you needed my help with?"

"Actually," he adds, bending down and extracting a few files from his drawer. "I need to get this up to Mr. Barbati, but I've got Mr. Yates coming in, and I'm afraid to miss him. Could you pay attention to see if he arrives in my absence and just let him know I'm coming?"

I know what is to be expected of me. I should be delivering those papers. I'm the assistant, after all. What strikes me as odd is that Mr. Hoffman isn't even suggesting it.

"Why don't you let me take them upstairs?" I ask.

"Oh, but what about your-a... your elevator issue?"

I appreciate the way he expressed is so nicely. What I don't appreciate is everyone here knowing about it. But I guess it's a pretty weird thing, and word of weird things tends to spread.

"The only way to beat a fear or an obsession of any kind, is to face is straight on," I shrug.

Although I don't feel nearly as confident and calm about it as I sound, just thinking that I am makes it almost true.

"That is very brave of you," he smiles at me benevolently.

"It's either that or changing my workplace," I chuckle.

"Oh, no, no, we can't have that," he shakes his head reluctantly at me, so hard that his glasses slide down his nose. Gently, he pushes them back up. "We absolutely can't."

"I think so, too," I agree. "I like this place too much."

"And I think I speak for everyone here when I say that we like you, too."

"That's very nice to hear, thank you, Mr. Hoffman," I appreciate his fatherly demeanor more than I thought I would. "As for now, I can take those documents up to Mr. Barbati."

He seems to hesitate for a moment, then hands me the documents.

"They're all signed and sealed," he adds.

"I'll let him know," I'm already up from my seat, strangely exalted.

I'm not going to see him because I gave in. I'm just doing my job. And those thoughts lull me into a false sense of safety that allows me to use the elevator, with my eyes closed of course, and get out on his floor.

This time, more than ever, I feel the palpitations of my heart loudly in my ears. I don't know what's going on. I've never felt this way about anyone before. Then again, Rocco Barbati isn't just anyone.

A wave of heat washes over me, reminding me of his skilled touch and how I moaned his name breathless, begging for more. But this is my workplace. His workplace, too. We need to act like professionals and prove that we can keep our private lives separate from our work.

I knock on the door confidently, my hand a fist.

"Come in," he shouts from inside.

I do as he instructs. Just like that first time I came up to his office, he's huddled over his desk. His laptop is in front of him, and I hear the quick tapping on his fingers on the keyboard.

His raises his gaze to meet mine, and immediately lights up upon seeing me. He's dressed immaculately in a crisp, dark grey suit, with a yellow tie. The combination looks amazing on him. His hair is sleek, slid to the left side, framing his face perfectly, and yet opening it up. I notice he hasn't shaved, and somehow, he looks even better with some facial hair – if it was even possible for him to look any better than he already has.

"Grace," he smiles. "Couldn't keep away, huh?"

"You wish," I chuckle, deciding to play his game.

Honestly, I didn't know how this would play out. A part of me was even upset, thinking that he could have changed his mind about getting together again, leaving me in such an unenviable position of giving me a taste, but not fully satiating my hunger.

"Mr. Hoffman sent me up to bring you these," I walk over to his desk and place the documents on it.

"How very serviceable," he chuckles, getting up. "Also, convenient. I've been meaning to call you."

"I bet," I try to mask my disappointment at his words. If he wanted to call, why hasn't he?

"Doesn't feel nice to keep waiting for someone to call, does it?" he suddenly says, and at that very moment, I know exactly what he's trying to do. He's giving me a piece of my own medicine. I said I wanted to call about the chocolates, but I didn't. OK, Mr. Barbati. Nicely played.

"Something to drink?" he asks, walking over to a cupboard in the corner.

I enjoy the view of his body gliding so effortlessly across the room. His broad shoulders are perfectly accentuated in that suit, and those trousers with that crisp line in the middle made the flexing of his ass painfully prominent. How gorgeous could someone be?

"No, thank you. I have to get back to work," I explain, shaking my head, although there's nothing I'd rather do than stay with him here all afternoon.

"What strong work ethic," he says with his back turned to me.

I hear the sound of clinking. Probably ice in a glass. Then, he turns around and he's holding his drink in his right hand.

"Just one drink, I won't tell," he winks.

"I would, but the boss is an asshole," I chuckle. "I don't know what he would do if he found out."

"Oh, I see," he takes a sip from his glass, then continues to walk over to me.

The very sight of him feels like a nice hot shower after a long day. It's impossible not to have your awareness of him heightened to crazy degrees. When I'm this close to him, I have no idea what we are. The line is dangerously blurred, and I'm afraid I could fall in deep, too deep to ever be able to come back for air.

He is standing right in front of me now, his knees authoritatively pressed between mine, as he pushes me all the way back to his desk. I put my open palms on the cold, hard surface for balance.

"Your boss sounds awful," he clicks his lips upon another sip.

With that look, there is nothing he couldn't demand, nothing he wouldn't get. I feel caged in by his presence, by his invasion of my personal space, and yet, I don't budge. This is exactly where I want to be.

"He totally is," I nod, enjoying the game. At this point, I don't even care that it's completely obvious what kind of an effect he has on me. It's undeniable. It's full and complete. My body is strained towards his, pulled towards his by an invisible force field.

"But you like it... just a little?" he whispers, his nose nuzzling my earlobe, inhaling deeply. "God, you smell good..."

A surge of arousal grips me wildly. His cologne is overpowering, omnipresent. I look into his eyes and I see only heat and hunger there. It feels as if I'm looking into a mirror, and it is only showing me my own wants and needs.

Do I want him? Crazy so.

Is it bad for me? Hell yes.

Do I care? Not one freaking bit.

"We shouldn't be doing this..." That's all I manage to say, feeling his tongue brush against my ear. His hot breath nuzzles my neck.

"There's many things in life we shouldn't be doing," he whispers, with a mischievous chuckle.

His hands dig into my ass, and now I'm seated on his desk. His cock, hard and palpitating, is pressed against my inner thigh.

"I have to go," I keep talking, but it's all in vain. My own body isn't listening to me, and neither is his. "There's work to be done..."

"Just one kiss," he murmurs.

"We both know it won't end with that."

But he's not listening. Panting softly, he seals his lips over mine, gently and passionately at the same time. I sigh under the strain, as his tongue darts inside, ready to explore, demanding more, demanding all I have to give. He's not as aggressive as the previous time, but I'm equally turned on.

Without even thinking, my hands dig into his hair, guiding his head. I hear his moan into my lips, his cock even harder against my thighs, begging to be let out. He deepens the kiss, claiming every part of my body as his, and we haven't even had proper sex.

Proper sex... The though makes me smile, but I'm too focused on my raging heartbeat. Our chests clash against each other, my breasts heaving, longing for his touch. It's crazy, but there's nothing I can do but succumb to his will.

"I want you so much, Grace..."

I kiss him back as fervently as he kisses me, as if stopping would mean our very death. My clit wakes up, tingling with the memory of his fingers, of his lips and tongue, begging for a repetition of what happened.

His hands still on my buttocks, gripping into me, he pushes me onto him. He slides one hand up my silk stockings and under my skirt.

"Oh, God, Rocco..." I gasp, moaning in pleasure, in anticipation of the pleasure yet to come.

"I like the sound of that," he whispers, his voice deep and breathy.

I can feel myself bare from the waist down, my skirt pulled up to my waist. He lifts his gaze to meet mine, fire burning, threatening to undo us both. I spread my legs to accommodate him, my fingers still raking through his hair, the room around me spinning as if we were in the middle of an earthquake.

He bites my lower lip, groaning. I feel the tip of his finger on my underwear. He's so close. He's so...

"Mr. Barbati?"

The sound of his secretary on the intercom interrupts our moment of mindless passion. As if someone spilled a bucket of ice-cold water over us, he pulls away from me, my lips feeling a painful emptiness where his once were. He uses the tip of his thumb to wipe his lips.

Slowly, he walks over to the other side of the desk, pressing the button.

"Yes, Victoria?" he replies, still breathless.

"Mr. Hanson is here."

"Fuck," he says, and I chuckle.

But I guess that was only for me to hear. His finger was off the button that time. Then, it lowers itself once more.

"Tell him I'll be ready in a minute."

"Of course, sir."

"You're lucky Hanson's here," he grins, walking over to me and giving me a peck on the lips. "Tonight?"

"Sorry, I got plans with Alisa," I shake my head.

"Tomorrow night?"

"I also have plans with- "

"You're a very busy girl," he tilts his head, but doesn't sound annoyed. "Maybe I'll just come steal you in the night then."

"You can try," I chuckle, sliding off the desk, and straightening my skirt.

"I can't help it. You're driving me crazy."

"Then some space will do us both good," I wink, blow him a kiss, and walk out of his office.

My heart is beating like crazy, but I did it. I won the battle.

Sort of.

Chapter 22

Grace

The following day passes quickly. I had no reason to go up to Rocco's office, but he did send me another box of chocolates, and this time I did end up calling him back. I couldn't resist. He made me promise to see him tomorrow night.

But, for this evening, I already had plans. I knock on Mr. Hoffman's door a little after 6, and he says to come in. I catch him buried in some paperwork, which always surprises me, as it's not really his job. It's mine, or the guys over at finance should double check it all, and not him. But he always says he doesn't mind. It's his job and he wants to do it well.

"Are you done?" I ask with a smile.

"Yes, just finished," he replies, huddling the papers together in a neat pile, then sliding them over to the side.

"I have to say, I'm hungry," I say more for the sake of polite chit chat than being actually hungry.

"Me, too," he nods.

"Should we wait for your wife, or is she meeting us there?" I inquire.

"Well, actually," he suddenly looks up at me, then rakes his fingers through his hair, all the way down to the back of his neck. "She called about an hour ago to let me know that she's not feeling all that well."

"Oh, I'm very sorry to hear that."

"Yeah, what can you do. These things happen," he shrugs.

"Well, it's no problem to reschedule," I smile. "We can have this dinner some other time, when she can join us."

"I've gone ahead and made the reservations for three, and I'd hate to cancel like this, at the last minute. Helen told me she's fine with just the two of us going this time, and she'll join us next time," he says it casually, as if we were friends.

But I'm not sure how I feel about this idea of having dinner with my boss alone.

"I don't know..." I hesitate.

"Come on, it's just dinner," he smiles. "Besides, Helen loves these little garlic breads they have at this place, and I promised I'd pick her up some when I head home."

I'm still thinking, wondering about it. But then I hear Alisa's voice inside my head. I'm overthinking things again. Helen wasn't planning on getting sick. And it is true that canceling a reservation half an hour before you're supposed to come doesn't leave a good impression and it's definitely not a nice thing to do.

"Well, alright then," I finally make up my mind, smiling.

"Great!" he beams. "Let's get going then."

About half an hour later, we reach the restaurant both in our separate cars, and we're being seated by the waiter.

"I'll be right back with your menus," he tells us. "In the meantime, what can I get you to drink?"

"I'll just have some sparkling water for now," I say with a nod.

"Same," Mr. Hoffman adds.

"Very well," the waiter confirms, then leaves us.

I look around. It's a cozy little place, with mostly dark red and burgundy color overpowering the walls and the carpets. There are candles everywhere, even the chandelier is antique looking, only the candles are electric, just shaped cleverly. Overall, it's a nice place, although I can't escape the feeling that it is somehow set up for couples. There are heart shaped vases on each table, with a single red rose.

But, then again, I'm overthinking. It's just a restaurant with food. Nothing else.

"So, how do you find the big boss?" he suddenly asks, eyeing me from across the table.

"Rocco?" I ask, then I correct myself. "Mr. Barbati?"

"Yes," he nods, although I'm sure he didn't miss my overly familiar reference.

"He's... it's hard to settle on one word to describe him," I smile. "Have you worked for him long?"

"Almost ten years," he replies.

At that moment, the waiter brings our waters, and two menus, then leaves again politely, with a smile.

"What do you think of him?" I ask not because I particularly care, but simply because I don't know what to talk about, so it's safer to just stick to business related topics.

"I knew his father, God rest his soul," he explains. "He was a good man. His son... well, let's just say he doesn't share the same family values."

"What do you mean?"

"Oh, it's not for me to spread gossip," he waves his hand dismissively. "Now, let's see what to order."

Without a single more comment regarding Rocco, he opens the menu and starts browsing through dish names. I do the same, although I'm curious to hear what exactly he meant. Hopefully, there will be another chance to ask him.

The waiter comes a minute later, and we order. I take a sip of my water, and notice that Mr. Hoffman is staring at me.

"Is anything the matter?" I ask.

"The matter? No, no," he shakes his head, smiling. "I'm sorry, I was looking through you, not at you. Just wondering about Helen."

"Well, we could quickly eat then leave," I shrug.

"Oh, no," he assures me. "I'm silly. She's got her sister looking after her if she needs someone. But from what she's told me, it's just a minor cold."

"That's good," I nod. "Not that it's good that she's sick, I mean, just that it's a minor cold." I explain, feeling a little awkward at this point, for some reason.

I should have insisted on taking a rain check on this dinner.

"Have you been married long?" I ask in an effort to kill time before the food arrives and we won't need to be focused so much on the conversation.

"Quite," he nods. "Twenty years."

"Wow, that's a long time," I reply, amazed. "I hope that when I get married, it'll be just like that, for life."

"Do you plan on getting married soon?" he asks.

I don't take it personally. Besides, the idea of getting married to Rocco is as silly as expecting to have a tiger as a pet and it being considered safe practice. Ridiculous.

"No, not soon," I shake my head with a barely audible sigh.

"Why not?"

"I'm not really seeing anyone right now," I shrug.

"A beautiful woman like you not having anyone?" he pretends to be all shocked, and it makes me smile. "How can that be?"

"You're very kind to say that, but unfortunately, being in a relationship entails much more than just good looks, as you know, I'm sure, being married for so long."

"I do know," he nods. "My Helen has always been a beauty. Killer eyes. Legs for miles. Body of Venus de Milo. But I think it was exactly this beauty that made her think things in life come easily to those who are pretty."

"Oh, I'm sure it's not like that," I reply.

"It is, it is," he corrects me. "So, sometimes, it's hard talking to her about stuff, because she expects to be allowed to do exactly what she wants."

"Well, I'm sorry to tell you, but that's all women, not just your wife," I chuckle, and he joins in.

"Then, I'm screwed whatever I do, huh?"

"I think so," I laugh.

At that moment, our food arrives, and we start eating, only occasionally taking a break to comment on something unimportant. He then orders the garlic bread for his wife, and we walk out of the restaurant together stopping at the traffic lights, because I parked my car across the street.

"Thanks for the dinner," I say.

"It was my pleasure," he replies. "Next time I promise it will be more fun, because Helen will be with us. Out of the two of us, she is the one people invite. I'm just the tagalong."

"I had a nice time," I chuckle at his words. "Please, say hi to Helen from me and wish her a speedy recovery. I'm looking forward to meeting her soon."

"She is, too," he nods. "Only, I guess it wasn't meant to be tonight."

"That's OK, there is time," I smile. "Well, good night then."

"Good night, Grace," he says, then wraps his arms around me and hugs me tightly.

For a moment, I'm confused, totally taken aback by his gesture. But then I hug him back, patting him a little awkwardly on the back. He quickly lets go, gives me a meaningful glance, then waves and heads to his car.

I do the same, wondering about that hug, but finally opting to forget about it. Maybe he thinks we're friends now or something.

Chapter 23

Rocco

When I bring Grace over to my place, I realize she's definitely not in a good mood. There is a frown on her pretty face, something I don't like to see. The devil on my shoulder tells me I shouldn't care. We're not dating. We're not in a relationship. I shouldn't care one bit about what happens to her outside the hours that she spends in my arms.

But that's not how things ended up. She's invaded my every thought, and I can' do anything without her being there, in the back of my mind. I did what I promised myself I would never do. I fell in love.

"You OK?" I ask her, as she's sitting on the couch.

I've been planning on pouring us some wine, playing some music to get her in the mood, to make it special for her, but I see she's distracted, sitting there on the couch like a wet kitten.

So, I do what I never thought I'd catch myself doing with a woman. I sit by her side and put my arm around her. She doesn't stir. She just sinks into my embrace, and it feels strangely soothing.

"I am, just..." her voice trails off.

"What is it? You know you can talk to me about anything."

"I know, but..."

"But, what?"

She sighs heavily. She looks burdened by something.

"Just tell me, whatever it is, and we'll figure it out together," I urge softly, as she cuddles.

"Honestly, I'm not even sure if it's anything," she shrugs.

"It's obviously something if it's got you feeling this way."

"I got an email," she suddenly says. "Actually, two."

I wait for her to continue, not urging her. Whatever it is, I want her to tell me on her own, not because I'm making her. So, I wait. She gazes somewhere at the wall, that look of worry still on her face.

"The first one just said stay away from him, nothing else. Then, the second one repeated that same thing, only added that bad things would happen if I don't do as I'm told."

I frown. Someone's threatening her? Over me?

"Honestly, I didn't want to tell you, so you wouldn't worry, but- "

I take her chin with the tips of my fingers and I make her face me. Her eyes are a little watery. She looks sad, and all I want to do was cover that sad face with kisses, until she is smiling again.

"I want you to tell me everything. Everything. I want to know everything about you, what makes you smile, what makes you sad, everything."

"But why?" she wonders.

I look at her incredulously.

"Are you serious?" I ask. She nods softly. "Because you're incredible. You're unlike anyone I've ever met before, and I'll be damned if I lose you."

"But, what about no dating, and no getting closer?"

"Fuck that."

She laughs.

"There we go," I smile. "Now, those emails."

Just as quickly as she smiled, she reverts to apprehension.

"I don't know who could be sending them."

"I do," I sigh, remembering Sonya's visit to my office.

Could this be what she meant? Does she really think that she would achieve anything by threatening Grace?

"Who?" she asks, but I get the feeling she already knows. Me saying it would be just a confirmation.

"Sonya."

She lowers her gaze. She's thinking. Probably rewinding her mind, trying to see if she could have seen this happening.

"I still can't believe it," she whispers. "Why would she do this?"

"Some people are just like that," I shrug. "Entitled. When they don't get their way, they behave like spoiled brats, and they don't care who they hurt in the process."

"But I haven't done anything to her," she continues, sounding incredulous.

"You know it, and I know it, but she doesn't. She came to my office, trying to... I don't know, win me back, I guess."

"Do you want to?" she falters as she speaks, and I know why. She's been bitten by the jealousy monster. I like the idea of that.

"No," I shake my head, assuring her. "If wanted anything with her, I would have done it by now. I was honest with you, Grace, when I told you about her. It was just a one-night stand. Nothing more."

"But she obviously wanted more."

"That's not my problem," I snort. "She did this before. She'd barge into my office during the day. Poor Victoria almost had a heart attack seeing her approach. Eventually, when she saw that it wasn't provoking the response she hoped it would, she stopped."

"What made her do it again?"

"No idea," I say, watching the corners of her eyes crinkle. "Maybe she didn't like seeing us together at La Bella Cucina. Who knows what triggers crazy people?"

A line of worry appeared between her eyebrows.

"Is she dangerous?" she asks, still undecided.

"I doubt it," I reply. "She's been pushed more than this before, so if there was a breaking point for her, it would have happened by now. No, I think she just doesn't know how to handle her anger and dissatisfaction. She gave me those liners like you're mine or no-one else's, if I can't have you no one will... that shit. But, the point is, she just likes the attention it provides. The worst thing you can do to such people is ignore them."

"Well, that's a bit hard..."

"I know, especially when they're all in your face, or sending you unpleasant emails. I guess we'll just have to make sure to keep you safe."

"How?" she wonders, as her head nestles on my shoulder.

She feels like a little kitten taken off the street. You expect her to start purring at any moment. A loose strand of hair falls over her face, and I push it behind her ear with my hand.

I have no idea how she did what she did. She made me want her more than I ever wanted anything else in my entire life. And, not only that, but she's also made me want to have it all the time, not just once.

"Well, first course of action is not letting you go home tonight," I grin.

She chuckles.

"I like the sound of that..."

"I was hoping you might," I get closer to her, as she lifts her head.

Her lips look so kissable, and I can't resist.

Chapter 24

Grace

When he kisses me, it's hard not to be aware of the acute sexual tension between us. I try breathing him in, telling myself to take it slow, but it's impossible. He intertwines his fingers with mine, that simple touch just adding more fuel to the fire of lust.

He pulls me up and adjusts me comfortably over his lap, his lips still pressed to me. I feel every inch of him underneath me, hard and throbbing, and I know that this time I won't be satisfied with just his fingers.

My hand digs into his luscious curls, tugging at them, as I kiss him back with every breath I take. Now that nothing is between us any longer, I'm free to do what I want, what I've wanted to do all along. The way he kisses me is powerful and gentle at the same time, like the soft summer rain which promises a storm in the distance, and you can't wait for the cool shower to wash over you.

I suck on his tongue, as his hands traverse every inch of my body. He quickly slides my blouse over my head, our lips separating for only one brief second, then slamming hard against each other once more. I shift a little in an effort to straddle him better, feeling the strength of his erection underneath me, yearning for it.

My skirt is already on my hips, just like the previous time, only now, there is nothing that would interrupt us. My knees squeeze the sides of his hips as I grind into him harder, my kiss becoming deeper and more frantic.

I moan against his lips, as he strokes my tongue with his, biting on my lower lip, tugging at it, teasing me. His hands dig into my waist, as he bucks into me, his chest heaving heavily. We're both breathless, completely in the moment. The rest of the world seems to have wasted away, and there is nothing left but us.

He cups my face with his hands, bringing our foreheads close together, his lips pulling away.

"You are driving me crazy..." he groans, while my fingers trail the lines of his rock-hard muscles.

The pure rawness of his words makes me even hotter for him. I want to please him in every way possible. I want him any way he wants me, just so I can reach deep inside of him and see him, the real him he's been keeping hidden from the rest of the world.

My panties are still on, but that doesn't prevent me from stroking myself with his cock, sliding forward then backward, watching him close his eyes in ecstasy. I prop myself up on my knees, only to reach down to his nether region. I find his fly easily, unbuttoning it and pulling the zipper down. He adjusts for the sliding of his pants, then sits back down on the sofa.

"I need you, Rocco," I whisper, not feeling even slightly embarrassed at saying this out loud.

His back arches and he leans backward, allowing me to proceed. I release his glorious cock from the constraint of his pants and underpants, squeezing him gently. He hisses through clenched teeth, a sound which drives me crazy, making me intoxicated with the sight of him, with the smell of him.

My touch is still soft, teasing, as I slide up and down his length, feeling how hot and hard he is for me. My breath catches feeling his entire body shiver under my touch. But I don't stop. He doesn't want me to. I don't want to.

He suddenly opens his eyes and leans downward, towards his pants. He fumbles to reach the back pocket, extracting a condom wrapper.

"Always prepared, huh?" I chuckle.

"You know it, baby," he grins, tearing the wrapper open with his teeth.

He rolls the condom on skillfully. Once he's done, his finger trails the line of my tights, but he can't reach what he wants to reach.

"You won't mind, right?"

"Mind what?" I wonder.

Quickly, he tears a hole in my stockings, right between my thighs.

"What are you doing?" I chuckle, my hands around his neck.

"Exactly what you want me to," he replies, as his finger finds the thin line of my thong.

He slides it under my panties, trailing my lips.

"You're so wet..." he mutters softly, sliding his finger inside slowly.

I bite my lower lip, knowing what will follow. I can' wait. I'm shaking, my entire body trembling with anticipation. His fingers make me even wetter, our lips locked in an embrace of violent passion.

Suddenly, I grab his hand and move it to the side of him. I lift myself onto my knees, hovering just over his cock. He reads my mind. His hand slides down and removed my thong to the side, opening up the passage. Then, he rests them onto my hips, allowing me to dictate the rhythm.

I lower myself only enough to feel his tip. Erect and full, I whimper at the sensation. What he's done to me before will be nothing compared to what will happen now. I haven't even realized how aching for him I'd been until the moment I feel his cock between my legs. My craving went unfulfilled – until now.

One of his hands flies up to clench at my breast, my entire body tingling from the thick air around us, a heavy, overpowering mixture of desperate ache and pheromones. I lower myself a little more, hearing him gasp with pleasure. Little by little, he slides in deeper and deeper, my clit unable to handle the pressure.

"God, you feel so tight..." he moans in delicious torment.

His cock stretches me more and more, as I sit down onto him fully, taking all of him inside of me. My clit is desperate for attention, and he seems to be able to read my mind in this insane moment of absolutely no rational thought. His thumb presses against the palpitating button of my passion and starts rubbing if gently, in rhythm with my motions.

I inhale deeply, loudly, arching my back and closing my eyes. The entire world is an explosion of colors and sensations, as I fuck his magnificent, muscular body sprawled underneath mine.

When I open my eyes, I meet his in a promise that didn't have to be said or exposed in any other way than this. I slid down smoothly onto him, wet and slippery, reaching the very root of his being. My pleasure ripples all around his exquisite manhood which threatens to shear me in two any moment.

But I don't stop. I can't stop even if I wanted to.

I feel his fingers on my skin, his wet lips on mine. Little droplets of sweat are starting to appear on his forehead. His hips lunge into mine, adding to the delectable friction.

"Don't stop..." he whispers, and his voice pushes me beyond the limits.

Completely connected on a plane far beyond this one, wild and eager for him, I keep moving, grinding, gyrating like a fucking machine set on full blast. This ferocious need is too much, and I just have to keep going, until the very end, if it means my own undoing.

He comes quickly, in wild ecstasy, completely losing control, his beautiful face distorted by too much sensation. His lunges into me hard for that final thrust, and I follow him immediately, as his needy eyes drink me in. Spasms which seem to be rooted at my very core split my body, my heart, my mind in two, laying me bare and vulnerable for him.

Breathing heavily, I fall onto him, and he wraps his arms around me. We stay like that for what seems to be a small eternity, silent and motionless. When I finally lift my head, he cups my chin once more and kisses the tip of my nose. A wave of warmth splashes over my heart, and I know what it is. It is what I promised myself wouldn't happen. Not with him. But it happened. And now, there is no turning back.

"That... was amazing," I manage to mutter, removing myself from his lap and sitting instead next to him, with my head still on his shoulder and his arm around me in a loving embrace.

"It sure was," he nods softly.

I look down at my pantyhose. Torn. Very noticeably so.

"How am I gonna go home looking like this?" I chuckle, realizing that the best choice would be just to throw them away and go home just wearing my skirt and shoes, minus the pantyhose.

He looks down at me with a frown.

"I thought you were spending the night."

"I didn't think you were serious about that."

"You know me by now, Grace," he corrects me. "I never say what I don't mean, unless it's very obviously a joke."

"Well, that's very sweet of you, but I do sleep best in my own bed. Plus, I'm a blanket hog," I smile.

"I'll get you a blanket to yourself, don't worry. But I can't let you go home. Not after you've told me about those emails Sonya's been sending you."

I look at him. There is worry on his beautiful face, and it softens his usually sharp and serious overtones.

"Like you said, she wants to frighten me," I reply. "But I don't want to give her that power over me. If she wants to do something to me, then she can bring it. But, sending those emails is just childish, and I won't have it. I won't be controlled like that. I appreciate your concern and especially your offer to have me spend the night, but, no."

"You do know what that means for me, right?"

I said all that, but I haven't taken into account what that really entails. Not dating probably meant that he didn't do sleepovers. Offering me to do that must be a big step for him. But, if I do that, I will reach the point of no return. I'm close to it now, but maybe I can still shield my heart from hurt and getting broken. What is to guarantee that he won't grow bored of me like he did with all those girls before? There is absolutely no such guarantee, and I don't want to make that last step. No.

"I know," I finally reply, watching his gaze linger on mine. "Trust me, I know the importance of that step. But... I can't."

I get up and slide my pantyhose down, crunching them up then placing them inside my bag. I turn to him, and I realize that he's already walked over to me. He places his open palm on my cheek. It feels scorching hot to the touch.

"I understand," he says. "And I won't push you into anything. Just let me know when you get home, so I know you're home safe and sound."

"That I can do," I smile, kissing him on the lips sweetly. He still tastes a little salty. "And thanks for the offer."

"Sure," he smiles back.

He walks me over to the door, and I wave goodbye on the way out. I listen to the sound of his door closing, then enter the elevator down. The floor is there, luckily, but after what just happened, I can't focus on my fear. All I can think about are his hands on me, and how I never want him to let go.

The thought both thrills me and chills me at the same time.

Chapter 25

Grace

My drive home is quick, peaceful, and it allows me to gather my thoughts. I feel overwhelmed by what just happened, but at the same time, I don't remember the last time I felt this alive and happy. I know it's just silly old brain chemicals, but I can't forget the way his touch seared my skin, the way his lips pressed to mine, demanding me to give my all.

I'm afraid that if I let him, I will completely lose myself in this crazy, wild love. And, then if he leaves me, what will I be? Sonya, most probably.

I think of her once again, my hands firmly grasping the steering wheel of my car. I think of the first time we met, how she told me to keep the cycle of kindness going. Did she really mean it? I don't know. But I guess she couldn't have known that anything would happen between me and Rocco.

But nothing in life is an accident. Even if it seems like an accident when it happens to you, odds are the universe already has a preestablished idea of what should happen, and we, from our puny human points of view, are often unable to see so far into the future or even predict it properly.

So, her helping me and now, her scaring me into leaving him has to have some purpose, which I'm not seeing. In any case, whatever that purpose is, I will not succumb. I will not allow her to bully me into feeling scared to go out of my house or go to work. That is no life.

And, if she wants to take it a step further, then I'll be ready. But I can't have Rocco fighting my battles. I won't allow that. I'm not some damsel in distress and I want him to be fully aware of it.

Only, it's hard to tell him anything. I just want to gaze at him and keep quiet and keep kissing him. Nothing else. Unfortunately, life doesn't consist of only those kinds of pleasures. Life is a bit rough sometimes, and I want to be sure that I can lean on myself first, and others later.

I turn left at the traffic lights. A few ladies of the nights are right on their corner, doing what they do best – accosting potential clients. While I was waiting for the light to turn green, one of them waved at me seductively. I just smiled and shook my head.

"Your loss!" she shouted at me, but by the time she finished that sentence, I was already pressing on the gas pedal, and speeding away.

I've never been afraid of this city, and I've been living in it all my life. One crazy ex will not change that.

I turn into my street, and a feeling of calm flows over me. It's one of the most peaceful streets in the city, even during the day, but especially during the night. I rarely return home this late at night, maybe during occasional outings with Alisa. Seeing how peaceful it really is makes me feel calmer about life.

Rocco left me feeling happy, but ecstatic kind of happy. While there's nothing wrong with that, I feel like what I need right now is a calm kind of happy, where I would know what to expect and who to expect it from. A part of me, a hidden part of me to be honest, felt like I could perhaps have that with him. But I know deep down he isn't the type for settling down with someone, despite what he himself may think. He's like a big child with a lot of toys at hand, and when he sees something new, something he's never had before, he seems to need only that and nothing else. It's just that most things are a passing fancy for people like him, and it would be wrong to fool myself into thinking that he could ever love me enough for me to remain interesting to him for the rest of our lives. He's just not the type.

Still, that doesn't mean that we can't have fun. Only, I'm walking on a fine line here, and I'm afraid that I've already crossed once or twice into the danger zone. If I do it one more time, I'm afraid I'll be lost, and I won't be able to find my way back. I'll be his. It's as simple as that.

I park my car with a sigh. You're overthinking things again, Grace. I scold myself just as Alisa would. I don't blame her. I could have had a pleasant ride back home just waiting to slump down onto my bed and sail off into slumberland. But, no.

Now, my mind is filled with images of what happened, thinking and rethinking things. What could be, what couldn't be, and what should never be. It's tiresome. Maybe I just need a good night's sleep to make things seem clearer in the morning.

I park my car across the street as I usually do, listening for the beeping sound of my car being locked. I cross the street looking both ways out of some force of habit, although the street is completely deserted.

I look up to my building. All the windows are dark. Alisa is either sleeping or maybe she decided to have a sleepover somewhere else. I fumble inside my bag for my keys, when suddenly I hear footsteps behind me.

"Excuse me," a hushed voice says. "Do you have the time?"

I turn around to see a hooded figure. I can't see its face clearly, because the streetlight is aimed right in its back, leaving the front part of its body in complete darkness.

"Yes, it's- "

But, before I can even look down at my watch, the figure lunges at me, and the sickly-sweet smell of chloroform fills my nostrils, forcing me to inhale, until the world goes completely dark.

Chapter 26

Rocco

Half an hour has passed when I check the clock on the wall opposite me. When Grace left, I couldn't sleep, so I got a glass, filled it with whiskey and played some jazz, just waiting for her call.

When I see how much time has passed, a part of me is immediately alert. She needs twenty minutes to get home. Maybe five minutes more, give or take, if the traffic is heavy. But it's nighttime. There's barely any traffic.

I take another sip of my drink, thinking I'll wait ten more minutes, then I'll give her a call myself. Fuck rules of the game. I'm done with these games. If I want to do something, I should be able to do it, without any fear that I'll be thought weak. I want to know if she got home safe.

I'm not happy about the fact she turned me down on sleeping over. There's more to that proposal than she knows, but fine. Maybe this is not the right moment to offer it. It's a big step. Maybe she's not ready for it, and I sure don't want to push her into anything. That will only drive her away from me, and that's the last thing I want. So, I'm more than willing to be patient with her. She's worth the effort, I know it.

The next ten minutes feel like ten hours. I watch the clock ticking away, the hands scraping against the background in a futile effort to go faster. If anything, the longer you look at them, the slower they move, as if they know that this will make it more painful. Only, time doesn't care. It doesn't care at all.

Nine minutes are done, and I grab my phone. I won't wait any longer. If she thinks I'm overbearing... well, we'll talk about it. I'll say I'm sorry. I'll explain why I did it. All I want is to hear she got home safe.

I dial her number. It starts ringing. Once, twice. Ten times. Then, it stops.

I swallow heavily, putting my glass aside on the little nightstand. I'm in no mood for drinks. When you call someone you love in the middle of the night and they're not picking up, you always think the worst. You think an accident happened. You think they were mugged, robbed, beaten, left for dead.

I honestly don't know why I'm so worried. It must be this new state of mind, of heart. Cliché, I know. But fuck it. That's exactly what this is. It's that fucking disease called love, and I caught it bad. Now, I have to pine on the phone, just to make sure she got home safe.

But I do. And her voice is the only thing that would pacify me right now.

So, I call again. Still the same effect. She doesn't reply.

OK, she might be in the bathroom, taking a shower. But why didn't she send a stupid message when she got home when I specifically asked her to?

Fuck.

I call the third time, all my metaphorical fingers crossed. But still nothing. She doesn't pick up.

I get up and go to my study. I don't even bother to turn on the light, and instead, just walk over to my desk and extract a small leather book from the third drawer. I walk back to the living room and start leafing through it.

Quickly, I find what I'm looking for. Alisa Richardson 555-389-276.

Next to Alisa's name, there are others, such as names and numbers of Grace's parents, and a few other relatively important people she has contact with in her daily life.

Was it wrong getting all this without her knowing? Absolutely. I have no excuse, and I won't even ask for it.

Once I hear Grace got home safely, I'll explain this, too.

I dial Alisa's number, and despite it being almost 3 am, she picks up.

"Hello?" She sounds sleepy and groggy.

"Hi, is this Alisa?" I ask as politely as I can, although the first question I want to ask is if Grace got home.

"Yes?" she confirms, but obviously has no idea who I am. Why would she?

"Hi," I repeat, "this is Rocco Barbati, I'm Grace's- "

"Boss," she interrupts me. "I know. Why are you calling me?"

Straight to the point. I like that.

"I'm just calling to see if Grace got home safely," I explain.

"I don't know," she replies, and an alarm sounds off in my mind. "I'm not home. I'm at my... friend's place."

I can spot a lie very easily when I hear one. But I don't care if it's her fuck buddy or friend. I just want to know where Grace is.

"I tried calling her, but she's not picking up."

"Maybe she's sleeping? You know, like the rest of us."

I clench my teeth at her rudeness. But then I remind myself it's me who's the rude one, waking people up at 3 am.

"She headed home over half an hour ago," I explain. "I asked her to call me when she arrived, but she didn't. And now she's not picking up."

"Well, if she said she would call, then she would."

"I know," I nod more to myself than to her. "I was hoping you were home, so you'd be able to check, but..."

"No, sorry," she replies. "I could go home and- "

"No, no," I refuse her offer. If anyone will be checking, that will be me. Right now. Besides, who knows where she is, she could be miles away. I could be there in less than twenty minutes if I step on it. "I'll go and check. It's no problem. And I'm sorry for waking you up."

"It's OK," she says. "I'm glad to hear you're a nice guy who wouldn't just brush it off."

I want to say thanks, but that wouldn't be fair. I didn't use to be this guy. I was the guy who sent girls home in the middle of the night, paying for the taxi and considering that a job done. I didn't need to hear they got home safely, which was what I should have done. I see that now.

"Can you just drop me a message when you get there and if she's home? Now I'm also a little worried."

"Sure thing," I reply. "Talk later."

I hang up and rush out of the apartment, just grabbing my keys. The night is chilly, especially if you're without a jacket, but I don't feel it. I jump into my car and head straight for Grace's place. When I get there, I see her car parked across the street. Immediately, my anxiety disperses. So, she did get home. But why didn't she message?

I look up. The windows are dark. Maybe, she got home and immediately went to bed. But why no phone call or even a message? That's what's been eating at me, and I know I won't turn around and go back home. Not now that I'm so close to her. I just need to see those lips say she's OK. Nothing else.

I walk across the empty street, illuminated by streetlamps, which don't provide enough light. It all feels a little eerie, especially with all the darkened windows around. I keep walking despite the chill in my bones and stop several feet before the entrance.

A silvery flicker of light on the pavement catches my attention. Squinting, I bend down and pick up a little handful of keys. In the middle, there is a miniature photograph of two smiling young women, their arms wrapped around each other, their cheeks pressed together. I recognize one of them immediately.

I turn the plastic frame around, reading the inscription.

To Grace, my BFF forever.

Chapter 27

Grace

When I open my eyes, it's dark. Only some light shines through the window, from the bright pink neon sign plastered against the wall of the adjacent building. I don't need to look around to realize that I'm in an unknown place. This is not my home. This is not any place I've ever known. It smells like sweat and piss, and to my horror, I realize the smell is coming from the bed I'm lying on.

I'm breathing heavily. It's probably because of the rag stuffed in my mouth. It's already wet, having soaked up my spit, and I breathe through the sick sounding squelches it releases with my every breath.

I try to jump up from the bed, but something tugs at me violently, and I don't even move. I look to my right and see the ropes around my wrists, tied to the headboard. I try to kick, but my ankles are equally restrained.

My most primitive drive kicks in. I'm scared, petrified, like an animal that is about to be hunted down. There is no protection for me inside this place. My survival mode awakens inside of me, but being tied up, it can do little but growl into the soggy rag in my mouth.

At that moment, something moves inside the room. To the side of the window, almost hidden amongst the long, heavy curtains, there is an armchair. And, inside that armchair, a figure. A dark figure. A hidden figure.

I muffle some curses, but none of it comes out properly. I'm feeling a numbing mixture of fear and anger, but I know one thing. She can hide all she wants. I know who she is, and I refuse to be afraid.

I tug violently at the rope a few more times, but it does nothing. Not even the bedframe shakes. It's sturdy, as if made to have someone tied to it. I look instead to the window again, trying to notice something familiar outside, if anything just to see where I am, whether it would be worth it to shout, would anyone even hear or pay any attention.

But I see nothing other than the neon sign, which pokes at my eyes painfully, so I am forced to look away. I try not to breathe through my nose, because the smell inside this room is horrible. So, I hiss the wet air through my mouth gag, no matter how unpleasant it is.

I look down at the bed. It's too dark to see anything really. I only see dark shadows, maybe stains. I'm disgusted by the thought that I'm probably in some mangy old motel, where people go to fuck whores, leaving all their body fluids on the bed for the next client who comes along. I almost gag, which intensifies the feeling of nausea due to the rag inside my mouth.

I start coughing through it, afraid that I might vomit into my own mouth and then be forced to swallow it. I try to make loud noises, pointing at my head, and the figure seems to get the message. It jumps from the armchair, still wearing that hoodie I remember from a few hours ago. Or was it days ago? I can't tell. I feel like I've been asleep for days, and I have no idea where I am or what time it is.

Its face is still concealed inside the darkness of the hoodie, but I see when it brings its finger to its lips.

"Shhh," it says like death when a dying person wants to plead for their life.

I nod, quickly, and miraculously, my mouth is free. I gasp for air, again that image of a dying person flashing before me. I inhale greedily, as if every breath could be my last. Until I get enough, I'm not even considering shouting for help.

A few moments pass, and the figure retreats back into the shadow once again. I can't see it almost, but I know its there, like a guardian angel, only it won't keep you safe. It will kill you, if you let it.

"Heeeeeelp!" I shout from the top of my lungs.

The figure jumps up, lunges at me and slaps me over the mouth. Warm, coppery saliva floods my mouth as I swallow heavily. The right corner of my lip is stinging. I lick it a little with my tongue, and the stinging sensation becomes a fire.

The figure extracts something from its pocket, then huddles over it. A moment later, I see a small piece of paper brought before me.

No shouting. Talk.

Then, it crumples the paper and throws it in the corner of the room. I nod. Shouting when you're being kidnapped is probably the least productive thing you can do. It pisses off whoever is doing this to you, and odds are, you're probably nowhere near where someone can actually hear you and come to the rescue.

So, talk it is.

"I don't see the point of you hiding," I sneer at the figure. "I know who you are."

The figure doesn't stir. It's still too dark from the lack of light. Even the things I can see are just blurry outlines, as if someone put a veil over your face and pushed you out into the unknown. Walk. Make sense of the world around you.

Quickly, the figure scribbles something else. I can't see it scribbling, but now I know that's what it's doing in the dark, because another piece of paper follows.

What's my name?

The question is simple. But why ask it?

"Why?" I snort, deciding to take as much control as I can over her.

Maybe showing her that I'm not afraid will make her rethink this stupid decision and whatever goal she meant to achieve by it. What? Keep me away from Rocco forever? As if.

My mind reminds me of the words Rocco forever. My heart jumps at the idea. It skips a beat. I races like a horse at the realization that, despite what I've been trying to convince myself of, I love him. I love him with every fiber of my being, and nothing would make me happier than having him by my side for that stupid, idiotic happily ever after.

But I made a mistake. I can't help but feel stupid at the knowledge that, had I accepted his proposition to spend the night, none of this would have happened. I would be sleeping in his bed, breathing in his sweet, masculine scent. And, in the morning? Who knows? But I wouldn't be here, breathing in sweat and piss.

"Does this make you feel good? Seeing me like this?" I demand as if it's not me tied to this bed. "You get some weird kick out of this?"

The figure shakes its head. But it doesn't write anything on its little notepad.

"Talk, dammit!" I shout.

The figure raises its hand to me, and I turn to the side, away from it, expecting a blow. It doesn't come this time. When I open my eyes, its hand is down.

"I know you're heartbroken," I continue, a little more calmly this time. "But, shit happens, you know? So, he doesn't want you, big whoop. There's about a million other guys who'd die for just one look from you, are you even aware of that?"

Some more writing, and I see the next paper.

What's my name?

The same as last one, which is lying crumpled in the corner, with the previous message.

"Why?" I repeat. "Why does your name matter so much? Why do you insist on staying in the dark when we both know who you are and why you are here?"

I have to get her out into the light, to get her to show herself to me. The fact that she isn't talking means she knows this is wrong, she knows she's not supposed to be doing this. Maybe I can appeal to the little sense left in her, but I need to see her for that. Eye to eye.

"Just turn on the light," I say. "Please. Talk to me."

The figure shakes its head fervently. I'm losing her.

"You know this is wrong, right?" I ask. "This won't end well. You still haven't done anything irreversible. You just slapped me. That's fine.

I've been slapped before. No harm done. But, if you take it further, I won't be able to help you."

The figure seems to ponder it a little, then another shake of the head takes over. It scribbles quickly, its whole body tensing, trembling. I can sense she wants to talk, but something isn't letting her. Could it be that she's been diagnosed with a double personality disorder? One personality being the good one, like the Sonya who helped me in the elevator and the other a crazy speech ex who can't accept that it's over? I've only seen those scenarios in movies, but this one fits the bill perfectly.

Only, in movies, the person who's been kidnapped always finds a way to get out. Me, on the other hand? I'm not so sure. These ropes seem pretty tight, and I can't even try to do anything with her in the room. Maybe if she gets out and I can try to bend my thumb inward towards my palm or break my thumb. That's an option, too.

"I need to pee," I say out loud, hoping that this will get her out of the room, in search of a bucket or something, or maybe I'd be so lucky as to have her untie me.

But the figure just shakes its head. Then, it walks a few steps back and returns to me, showing me a clean t-shirt and pants in its hands.

"So, I'm supposed to just pee on the bed?"

It nods.

"You're a bitch," I growl. "It's no wonder he dumped you."

Maybe not a good plan but playing the good doctor didn't get me anywhere. Maybe if I piss her off enough, she'd lose control.

It shakes its head again. Then, I see another message, a more detailed one.

Are you sure I am who you think I am?

When I read this message, my lips part. Is it possible that it's not Sonya? Rocco told me she went to see him in his office. She threatened me, twice over email. She didn't sign her name, but who in their right mind would sign themselves when sending threatening emails? No one. In their right or crazy minds.

It's her. It has to be her.

"I know who you are," I hiss. "Don't try to confuse me. Rocco told me all about you, how you went to his office, and how he once again, sent you away because he doesn't want you. And, if you think about it for just one moment rationally, you'd realize there's nothing wrong with that. It's not his fault that he doesn't want you, and it's not your fault that you still want him. But you can't go around kidnapping people because your love isn't reciprocated."

Another message.

Only part of that is true.

"Which part?" I scoff. "Stop writing already and talk."

The figure huddles over to write, but no message follows. Instead, I see it throw the entire notepad into the corner. The pencil follows immediately behind.

"You want to know who I am?" A voice fills the room, and it sounds strangely familiar.

Only, it doesn't belong here. It belongs to a completely different place, a nice place, a safe place, because he is a safe person.

The figure leans over to me, but I still can't see anything, only a pair of eyes which stare at my very soul, threatening to steal it and never give it back. I want to scream, but no sound comes out of my mouth. I'm petrified, because now I know I was wrong. I was so terribly, terribly wrong.

When the figure stretches its arm towards a small lamp on the nightstand by the bed, I already know what the light will reveal.

A demon in its own right. A wolf hiding among the sheep. There are no glasses, but I would recognize that face anywhere, because I've been looking at that face every day for several hours straight, laughing with it, talking to it, even agreeing to have dinner with it even when our original plans fell through.

When he switches on the lamp, light spills all around us, but it doesn't help make this place look any more pleasant. I see the dark yellow and brown stains on the bed beneath me. I see the neon sign even more prominently.

And, I see the face of my boss, looming over me like a vulture ready to dive in and feast.

Chapter 28

Rocco

Gripping Grace's keys in my hand, I slam the car door behind me. In a situation like this, there is one person in the whole city who would know what's going on. I drive to the outskirts, passing by the docks and heading almost to the edge of the woods.

The hangar is there. Looks more run down than a barn from the 1800s, but that's the point, to make people think there's no-one there. I don't see a single car around. Again, there shouldn't be.

I know I'm treading into dangerous territory, but it's the only thing I can think of. If anyone finds out I was here, my business is gone. Just like that. But I can't think about my business right now. Not when I don't know where Grace is, and she is in the hands of a crazy woman who might snap at any moment.

If she hasn't already...

A dark voice inside of me reminds me of that possibility, but I try not to think about it. I have to believe that Sonya is just angry, and she's just trying to scare both me and Grace. She wouldn't really harm her.

But I'll believe that when I find her, when I find them both.

I decided against going over to Sonya's place. There's no point. She wouldn't be that stupid to stay there. No. I need help finding her, and that needs to be help from the underground. No legal sources could track down a criminal.

I get out of the car and start walking over to the hangar. A few owls hoot in the distance. Apart from that, there is no other sound. Pitch dark. Completely silent. It's the place nightmares are made of.

I reach the door, and the moment I push it in, I hear the gun click.

I know exactly what to do. I raise my hands in the air. I'm carrying no weapons, but rough hands still search me, not minding any decency. Once satisfied that I'm clean, I'm pushed inside a big, empty room, with just a few carboard boxes in the corner. A few guys look curiously over at me, cigarettes hanging from the corner of their lips.

One of them approaches me, spitting to the side as he walks.

"Who are you?" he asks.

"I need to speak to Moreno," I say, realizing I'm seriously outnumbered, and they could just throw me out. So, I need to be careful.

"The fuck you do," the guy spits at me. "Who are you, motherfucker?"

"Tell Moreno that Rocco wants to see him."

"Rocco who?"

"And tell him I come to collect a service for the frogs."

"The what?" the guy squints at me.

Of course, he has no idea what I'm talking about. No one does. Only Moreno, me and those other two kids who knew better than to mess with Moreno after that.

Suddenly, one of the guys in the corner walks over to the spitting me, and whispers something to him.

"You sure?" he wonders, and the guy just nods. Then, he turns to me. "Stay here."

He disappears somewhere in the back, his path leading around the cardboard boxes and into darkness. He returns less than a minute later, nodding at me.

"He'll see you."

I swallow heavily heading where he showed me. When I enter the following room, I see it's the same. There's nothing in but concrete walls and concrete floors. Only one window which right now, isn't letting in any light, and I doubt it's much different in daytime.

But then I see it. There is an open shaft in the floor, with what seem to be stairs leading down. Hesitant, I walk over there and look into what seems to be an abyss of blackness. Clenching my fists, I go down, one step at a time.

The moment I reach the bottom, the whole place lights up and I see a long hallway. I remember someone once told me that this was an old military bunker back in the day, and now I'm sure it was. I keep walking along that hallway until I reach a door and go straight through it.

I see him immediately. He hasn't changed much. He's got the same thinning hairline he's always had, even as a kid of thirteen. That same Roman nose. That same hawk-like stature and a tendency for his body to lean forward. Overall, he's never been a ladies' man, something I hear has changed once he became the uncrowned lord of the underground.

"I thought it was a joke when Fico told me someone came to collect a favor for those frogs," he stands up from a chair, taking out a thick cigar from his mouth and dipping it into an ashtray on a table.

I look around and a see a few things which might make this place homier, like a coffee machine, a bed, a safe, a shitload of cash on the table, and I just interrupted his counting obviously. He walks over to me, eyeing me, as if to make sure it's really me.

"You look the same," he tells me, placing his hand on my shoulder. "You sold your soul to the Devil or what?"

"Sometimes, I think so," I smile back, doing the same to his shoulder.

We remain like that for a moment, then both of us let go at the same time. He takes his seat at the table, then gestures at the chair opposite him.

"A man's gotta keep a count on his wealth, no?" he says.

"I got an accountant for that," I get comfortable, not taking my eyes off him.

We were friends once. Best friends. But that was a long time ago. This man is not someone I know. How am I to be sure that he still values a promise given twenty years ago?

"Yeah, mine's too busy hiding all the side flow," he shrugs, biting on that cigar and speaking with it still in his mouth. "So, what makes you stir the sleeping monsters of memory with your request??

"One night, when half my life behind me lay, I wandered from the straight lost path afar," I tell him.

"Ah, Inferno," he beams. "My favorite."

"I know."

"It is the one you saved me for."

Suddenly, uninvited and violent, completely taking over, I see it all once more in my mind's eye. I see Moreno for the sweet, young boy he was. A boy who only wished to be left alone to read and write poetry, but who was always picked on for that. Beaten. Tormented. We were friends, but not that close for him to confide in me about this. Then, I saw it all with my own eyes. By the brook, I beat up one of the guys and stuffed a live frog into his mouth. I caught the other one and did the same to him. No one ever picked on Moreno again, and we were best friends after that. Shortly after, his parents moved away, and we lost touch. I knew who he had become, just like he knew who I had become. But, neither of us ever felt capable of approaching the other. Something always kept us apart. Until now.

"I gave you a promise," Moreno nodded, his pale grey eyes like the eyes of an old sage, wise but punished for that knowledge with the price of seeing. "And I still hold onto it. What it is that you need from me?"

I quickly tell him what's happened. He listens intently, his face alert, not moving. When I'm done, he nods only once.

"You have her photo?"

"Whose?"

"Tua grazia," he says.

"Don't you need a photo of the woman who kidnapped her?"

Moreno shakes his head.

"When you search, you search for the one who is lost, not the one who has taken."

I believe him on this one. Of the two of us, he's the one who has found more lost people than I. I remember that I left my phone in my car, but then a sharp jingle hits me. The keys.

I get them out of my pocket, and I slide the keys over to him across the table. He takes them, his fingers gripping the little framed photo.

"The one on the- "

Wordlessly, he turns the frame to me and points exactly at Grace. I nod, wondering how he knew immediately who she was.

"Bella," he says, glancing at the photo one more time.

"She is, and much more," I add.

He raises his eyebrow. Then, his lips spread into a wise smile.

"Can you find her?" I ask, pleading. "We don't have any time to spare. I would look for her myself, but I have no idea where to start even."

"There is no place in this city where I don't know what's happening," he assures me, and I know it to be true.

Moreno has been keeping a tight grip on the underground for years. Drugs, guns, money laundry. Anything but people. They say his connections in the police are so good that he's become untouchable.

He presses a button on his desk, and a loud buzzer is heard. The big guy, Fico, comes in and walks over to him. Moreno explains in a few words what is needed, and Fico grabs the keychain, leaving us again.

"I want to go with him," I stand up, but Moreno leans over the table and grabs me by the wrist.

"People will talk to Fico because they know he is my right-hand man," Moreno explains. "But even he will look suspicious if they see a stranger with him. Do you want to risk finding her?"

"No," I shake my head, feeling helpless.

"You've done your part. Now let me do mine."

I know that what he's saying makes sense. But it feels fucking debilitating sitting like this, with my hands crossed, not being able to do shit about this.

"So, I just sit here and wait?" I growl more at myself than at him. Luckily, it seems that he understands.

"As much as it pains you to do so, yes."

He stands up and walks over to a small cupboard, extracting a dark, wooden box. He puts it on the table and opens it for me. There are still three cigars left inside.

"Thanks, but I'm not in the mood," I shake my head.

"I have repaid my debt," he reminds me. "Take one."

I know what is expected of me. We need to seal the deal in a way, to make it official, for us both to acknowledge that his debt has been repaid. So, I reach out and take a cigar. I bring it to my lips, and he lights it for me.

I inhale deeply. The aroma clutches at my throat, but it feels good. It is some high-quality stuff, which even I find difficult to get. I don't question his sources. I probably don't even want to know. Just like I don't want to know whose legs he'll have to break to get the info I need. I don't care. I just want to find out where Grace is and to get there in time.

Moreno looks at me from across the table, his eyes the essence of wisdom itself. We're the same age, and yet, I feel like he's twice as old as I am. Maybe he feels the same way, having seen stuff I can't even imagine. At some point, we just started leading different lives, and our paths went their separate ways. Maybe they would have intertwined at some point, but they didn't. Until necessity made me search for him.

"How long will we have to wait?" I ask, taking a deep, satisfying puff.

"Not long," he mirrors my action.

"But what if she's in danger? What if I'm too late, by the time your goons come back with her whereabouts?" I can't remain as calm and impassive as he is.

I feel nothing but fear now. Adrenaline courses through my veins, eager for action, but I can't do anything at this point. There is a hurricane of thoughts inside my head, and none of those thoughts end well for Grace. She needs my help. I know she does.

Moreno stares at me, the fingers of his left hand gently drumming against the polished surface of the desk that separates us.

"He can that have patience can have what he will," he tells me.

An invisible clock ticks inside my head, like a bomb. But I know I must wait.

Chapter 29

Grace

I'm shocked, unable to say or do anything. Mr. Hoffman slides off his hood. There is no point in hiding anymore. The darkness is no longer his friend. It is no one's friend.

He rakes both of his fingers through his hair, turning away from me, and pacing about the room like a caged tiger. I don't know what to say, or how to react to this. My mind if a blank, and there is no ink to write the following chapters of my life story.

Only, I must do something. Anything.

I watch him as he circles the room, muttering something to himself. This isn't the man I know, the man I got to know as a boss. Could it be that I didn't see what was hiding under that calm surface?

"Mr. Hoffman?" I finally dare to say his name, not having the slightest idea of the effect it might on him. But I need to do something.

He turns to me. There is a flicker of a smile, but it a madman's smile. He walks back to me, and sits down on the bed, by my side. He looks at me deeply, almost lovingly, and I'm fighting the urge to vomit again. This just can't be. I've been pointing the finger of blame at the wrong person all along.

"You understand why I did this, don't you?" he asks me, nodding, as if expecting me to just nod, too.

His hand reaches out to me and caresses me gently on the cheek. He feels cold, slimy.

"I... I do, only I need more to understand truly why," I say, but the moment those words pass the boundary of my lips, a frown appears on his forehead, crunching it up.

His hand pulls away in disgust we both seem to share.

"Then, you don't understand," he tells me.

"But I want to understand," I assure him.

As long as we are talking, he won't hurt me. At least, that's what I'm hoping, because I don't know why he's got me here. But that look in his eyes is giving me a pretty good clue. Just the thought of it makes me sick.

"I'm sorry about..." he points at my lip, his fingers trembling.

He gets up and takes a towel from the kitchen. It is moist and smells almost as bad as the bed underneath me. He tries to wipe the corner of my mouth with it, but I keep jerking my head away from the repulsive cloth.

"I'm fine," I assure him. "I know why you did it. Because I didn't listen. Those who don't listen should be punished, in a way."

"Yes," he agrees. "But I didn't bring you here to punish you."

"Why did you bring me here?"

"You weren't listening to my advice," he explains, withdrawing the offensive towel from my sigh.

"What advice?"

Then, it hits me. Was he the one sending those emails, warning me against being with Rocco? The neon sign flickers more painfully, and I have to look away from it.

"He doesn't love you," he says with an unwavering shake of the head. "He will never love you. Not as much as..."

Him.

Now it is all starting to make sense. I doubt his wife was ever invited to that dinner. She probably didn't even know about it. And he made it seem too casual, lying so easily about the whole thing.

But there's little I can do about any of that now, lying tied up in some God forsaken place. I needed him to get out of the room, so I can at least try to loosen the ropes.

"I had no idea you felt that way," I start slowly. I have to be very careful going this way, because I might slip at any moment, and if I do, he will never trust me enough to leave me alone, even for a moment. "You were always very professional with me."

It is easy to lie because I'm actually not lying. I'm saying the truth. He really has been nothing but a perfect picture of professionalism and good manners, and I still can't believe that he is the person responsible for all this.

"I had to be..."

"Of course," I assure him I understand. "There was no other way, and you did exactly what you were supposed to do. That's why I'm finding it so hard to believe it was you who sent me those emails, trying to keep me safe."

Upon hearing those words, he raises an eyebrow. Maybe I'm saying what he wants to hear.

"I know you never meant any harm," I continue choosing my words very carefully, knowing this is my only chance. "How could you harm someone you love?"

His face lit up hearing me say that. He broke into a smile, a crooked, uneven smile which sends shivers down my spine. I fight my revulsion, and I smile back.

"You do understand," he whispers.

"How could I not?"

"I really didn't bring you here to hurt you... and these," he gestures at the ropes binding me to the bed, "these are in case you didn't understand, and you felt the need to escape."

"I know," I reply. "But I do understand. Maybe you could untie me?"

It was too soon for that. I can see it in his eyes, that flame of distrust rising, transforming into a smoldering blaze. I had him, but now I lost him. He won't trust me again no matter what I say.

"If you understood, you wouldn't ask me that," he hisses angrily.

He jerks back, getting up and pacing the room again.

"What would your wife say if she found out you did this?" I suddenly ask.

His body twitches, his back turned to me.

"What would your daughter say?"

He's silent. He won't turn to face me. Using the moment, I tug at the ropes, but all they do is dig into my flesh more tightly, leaving bloody, red marks on my wrists. It's impossible to slide my hand out, no matter how much I squirm.

He finally turns to me.

"Not like they would ever know," he tells me. "My wife left me and took our daughter with her."

A chilly realization washes over me. He's been planning this for a while. Even that dinner and how it turned out wasn't an accident. I finally accept the fact that I won't talk my way out of this. I will leave this room only if he allows me.

"I'm sorry to hear that," I say, feeling like I have nothing left to lose. "But that's got nothing to do with me. You're angry at the world, and you're taking it out on me."

"No, no," he shakes his head at me, grabbing at his temples. "You don't get it; you just don't get it."

He sits on the bed again, and I feel the sweaty palm of his hand on my cheek once more. It's even colder now, even clammier.

"You are so beautiful," he whispers. "You deserve to be loved. I can love you, if only you let me..."

He lowers himself close to me, and I can already smell his sour breath. Petrified, I know that a kiss won't be the only thing he will demand. I could see it in his crazed eyes, in the way he professed his love for me.

He lays his hand on my breast.

"No!" I shout at him, but his sour breath is on my lips and I feel him trying to shove his tongue into my mouth.

Chapter 30

Rocco

Stepping on the gas pedal, I rush over to the address written on a small piece of paper stuffed in my pocket. Moreno did his part. I had the address within the hour. I don't know how, and I chose not to ask. It didn't matter. What matters is that I have a destination to go to.

But something else worries me. Fico said that she wasn't with Sonya. A guy brought a girl who looked exactly like Grace, and she seemed unconscious to a sleazy motel. He said she was some hooker he picked up from the streets, and who just needed a place to sober up. The guy at the motel didn't question any of it. Of course, he wouldn't. He just collected the cash and turned a blind eye to whatever was happening there.

Passing through every red light, not stopping to wait for it to change, I drive like a maniac through the streets of the city. If a cop pulls me over, I'll just bribe him. There's no cop that's going to say no to thousands of bucks.

I finally reach the motel. The no vacancy sign is turned on, shining brightly. It's an old, worn down building in serious need of some renovation. A few of the windows gape at me with broken glass, like sore eyes. On the building next to it, there is a pink neon sign trying to poke my eyes out with its glare.

I barge into the motel. A guy of about fifty, grey hair, a few missing teeth and wearing a Bulls t-shirt sits behind the front desk. There's a small tv to his side. There's a basketball game on, which he's obviously been following. He checks me out from top to bottom, grinning.

"Ya lookin' fer a girl, mister?" he asks with a thick Southern accent.

"Actually, I am," I nod, taking out the keychain and showing him the photo of Grace attached to the keys. "This one here. I was told she was brought here by someone."

"Well, nah," he just takes a glance at the photo I'm showing, quick enough for me to realize that he did it only for show. "Ya can't expect me ta interrupt a girl who's workin.'"

"She's not a working girl," I growl at his self-satisfied, smug face. "She's my girlfriend and she was brought here against her will."

"No one was brought 'ere agains' their will, mister, I assure y- "

I grab him by the collar of his t-shirt and slam his head against the counter, holding him down with my other hand. My teeth are clenched, and I feel I could wring his neck.

"Listen here, you hick," I hiss down his throat ready to pounce on him for one wrong word and he knows it. "I will show you the photo of my girl once more and this time, you better have something for me, otherwise I will bring the police down your neck and have you locked up for the rest of your miserable life!"

"Twenny-three!" he shouts helplessly. "Room twenny-three!"

He lifts his left hand to point at a board with keys hanging on nails. On every key, there is a keychain with the number. A few keys are missing, one of them being twenty-three.

"Where's your spare?" I growl, pressing my fingers deeper into his neck.

"Here," he squeals, fumbling somewhere underneath the front desk, then slamming them in front of me.

"She better be there," I snarl at him baring my teeth.

I rush up the stairs. There are only three floors, but a long hallway spreads into two sides, with several doors scattered either way. I rush down the hallway on the second floor, and quickly find room number twenty-three.

With my heartbeat drumming inside my ears, I feel deaf. But I don't need to hear. I just need my eyes not to fail me. My eyes and my fists.

I don't even think before acting. I can't. It doesn't matter if there are a bunch of guys there or just one. I will take them all on.

I unlock the door quickly and kick the door open with a loud bang. The room is dark, and a figure is huddled on the bed over someone. I see bound hands and feet.

When the figure lifts its head to me, I feel paralyzed.

"Hoffman!?" I shout.

I see Grace's sweet face lying on the bed. She's as shocked as I am, her mouth agape at seeing me. Anger takes me completely over, this wrath that has been a part of me for hours, mixing with worry. I feel like I've swallowed a fire-seed and it's exploding inside of me, threatening to burn all those around me to ash. An awakening blossoms in my heart, a need more potent than any other I've felt before. A desire to protect the one I love.

Staring at me in disbelief, as if he didn't recognize me or his own name, he looks around. I'm standing in the doorway, so he can't run past me. Instead. He rushes for the window, but I jump with my arms around his waist, pulling him down onto the dirty, grimy carpet.

I straddle him, my knees are at the level of his shoulders and my full body weight is keeping him pinned to the ground. My fists clench on their own, fueled by anger. This wrath is no dysfunction. My quick reactions are painful, as my fists hit the target with each blow.

The first punch shatters his nose. Blood starts trickling everywhere, and he coughs, spitting up some. But he is rendered motionless, and there is nothing he can do about it. The second punch dislocates his jaw. He cries in pain, but that doesn't stop the blows. I punch him again and again, until I could only see the white of his eyes in the bloody mess of his face.

"Rocco!" Grace shouts and it is her voice that brings me back to reality.

I am no longer in Inferno. Her angelic voice pleads with me, and I am back.

My knuckles are stinging. They'll be sore as Hell tomorrow. But, for now, I don't feel any pain. Not now that I know she is safe.

I jump up from Hoffman, assured that he won't be going anywhere. I immediately start undoing the knots on Grace's hands, untying her completely. The reddened bracelets around her wrist infuriate me again, but one look from her assures me that she's fine. I came just in time.

She buries her face into my chest, breathing heavily. She sobs quietly, overcome by emotion. I allow her some time, gently caressing her silky hair.

When she raises her gaze again, her eyes are bright. There isn't a single tear in them.

"How did you find me?" she asks.

I look down. My childhood friendship with the current underground mob boss isn't something I intended on boasting about. But I don't want to lie to her. I never want to be unfaithful or untruthful with her.

"I had some help," I start. "But let's leave that for another time. I want to get you out of here and give that dirtbag what he deserves." I look to the side at the unconscious body on the ground.

Her eyes look at me all frightened.

"I won't touch him again," I promise. But I don't say anything else. She doesn't need to know that I already called the cops. Only, I didn't call the good cops. I called the bad cops, who don't mind breaking the law for a few grand, before taking this guy in. Again – she doesn't need to know any of this. All she needs to know is that Hoffman is done for. He will never be allowed to harm anyone again.

"How did you know it was Hoffman?"

"I didn't," I shake my head. "I went to an old friend for help, and he's got some... unusual connections." I opt for that version for the time being. If she wants to know more about it later, I'll share the whole story. "I wanted to show him Sonya's photo, but he was right."

"How?"

"He wanted your photo."

"You have my photo?" she asks, rubbing her ankles.

"I found your keys," I take them out from my pocket and give them back to her. Seeing them, she smiles, and the sadness of that smile breaks my heart. "But, come, let's get you out of here. I don't want to stay here a moment longer."

I pick her up in my arms, and she huddles close, like a slumbering kitten. She smells awful, just like this room. But I know the cure for that. When we pass the hick on the way out, he stumbles backward.

"Make sure the guy in twenty-three doesn't go anywhere, or I'll be back for you," I tell him.

He just nods quickly, unable to look me in the eye.

By the time I'm out of the building, Grace is already asleep. She looks so peaceful; she is pure love. I put her gently on the back seat. She stirs a little but doesn't wake up. Slowly, I close the door, and glance over at the building.

Two cars park in front, and a bunch of guys appear. I recognize one of them. The others are strangers. He looks in my direction. He nods. I nod back. Then, I get into my car and drive away. I don't care what happens to that shithole Hoffman.

I check Grace in the rear-view mirror. She is sleeping so soundly, with such a peaceful expression on her face, you'd never think this just happened to her. I step on the gas pedal and drive back to my place.

My mind is strangely blank. Empty. That anger is gone, and I'm overwhelmed with emotion for her. Even that fear that I could have lost her is gone, as if it was never there in the first place, and all I can focus on is Grace, keeping her safe and happy.

When we reach my place, and I take her back into my arms again. She opens her eyes sleepily. I see the dried blood in the corner of her lip, and I kiss it. She smiles.

"You came for me," she murmurs drowsily.

"Of course," I nod, letting our noses touch.

"I still can't believe it..."

Immediately upon entering my apartment, I put her on the sofa and go into the bathroom, to run her a nice, warm bath. I find some long-forgotten bath salts, adding them in. Fifteen minutes later, I watch her body dive under the water, welcoming the cleansing sensation.

I pour some shampoo in my hands, and wash her hair, gently raking my fingers, massaging her scalp. She closes her eyes.

"That feels so good..." she whispers.

"Just relax, baby," I tell her. "You've been through enough today. Let me take all of it away."

She suddenly opens her eyes and turns to me.

"What will happen to him?"

She is actually worried about that piece of shit. That's what a sweet, kind person she is, and I can't believe it.

"Does it matter?"

"I think something's wrong with him," she says.

"I'd say so, too," I nod, continuing to massage and wash her hair. She moans softly.

"I hope he gets the help he needs," she adds, her eyes still closed.

"I don't want to talk about him anymore," I shake my head. I don't want her to know that I wish him exactly the opposite. I hope he's unable to breathe properly after the guys are done with him. "I want to talk about you. Only you."

"I just want to go to sleep," she murmurs softly.

"Sure, the bed is ready," I nod. "I just wanted to give you a nice bath before putting you to bed."

She turns to me again, a few drops sliding down the side of her beautiful face. Her eyes sparkle like stars, like two flickers of a candle in the wind, refusing to go out even in a storm.

"Why are you doing this?"

Her eyes are looking at me, open and honest like a child's. All I see in them is warmth, a feeling of safety that is mine, only if I decide to accept it. They remind me of home, as blissful as the color of water when it blends into the blue of the sky, endless and unquestioning, just accepting.

Her face is relaxed, and every word she has communicated to me has been nothing but loving and full of trust. There is nothing standing between us any longer. Before, I would be looking for an exit out of such a situation. But not this time. Not with her.

The silence between us feels renewed. Her eyes still aglow, radiating with sunlight. There is only one thing I want now. Only one thing I need.

"Isn't it obvious?" I answer her question with another question.

The bubble foam slides down from her upper body, revealing her perfectly rounded breasts. Her pink nipples are perked up, and I feel a most tenacious desire to wrap my lips around them. But, if I do that, then she won't be going to sleep. She needs her sleep, now more than ever.

"No, I want to hear you say it," she whispers.

I cup her chin to face me. Her lips are glistening wet. I press mine onto them slowly, gently, taking my time.

"Because I love you," I say, our foreheads touching.

"I love you, too," she replies breathlessly.

"Come on now," I smile. "Let's scrub you down and take you to bed."

She nods, lifting her knees and wrapping her arms around them. She finishes with her bath and the moment her head touches the pillow, she falls asleep.

I lay down next to her, but sleep doesn't come. It doesn't matter. All that matters is that she is lying next to me.

Chapter 31

Grace

A week passes by in the blink of an eye. A part of me is still trying to process everything that's happened. I'm still in disbelief at how Mr. Hoffman managed to fool everyone, including me. But I guess it's easy to trust someone who is supposed to be your superior and who has never given you any reason not to trust him.

Rocco doesn't like the idea that I've returned to work basically after four days of our ordeal. He's assured me it wouldn't be a problem to take more time off, but honestly, I don't want to lock myself up in my apartment, with not even Alisa there during the day, and wallow in why this happened to me. It's just not who I am, and I don't want it to ever be me.

When I explained this to Rocco this way, I could see he understood where I was coming from. I was shifted to a different department, although my position remained the same. I just wanted to continue where I left off, and not give Hoffman another moment of my time or my thoughts.

That morning, I'm walking into the Visionetworks building as confidently as I can. Marc, the security guy, glances at my ID only because he has to, although he's already smiling at me and nodding.

"Morning, Grace," he greets me.

"Morning, Marc," I smile back. "How are the wife and kids?"

"The baby is keeping us all awake, but we're surviving somehow," he chuckles.

"Well, it's the baby's job to get you all in line," I laugh, walking through the passageway, which clears me with a ping.

I'm a bit early this morning. I want to get started right now, so I can skip work early, too, and head over to Rocco's. It's his birthday, and I have something special planned for him. He even offered to let me have the day off if I wanted, to what I replied that it's his birthday not mine.

I'm approaching the elevators, and that familiar knot in my stomach starts to form. You'd think that after everything I've been through, I'd at least be able to ride the elevator more calmly, but no. The knowledge that I'll get to see those wires again makes me nauseous and dizzy before I even enter the big sardine can.

But, before I can even press the button to call for it, I see it coming down on its own. I take a step back, expecting someone to exit. The door opens, and sure enough, a person comes out. A familiar person, carrying a box of stuff, her face a mixture of anger, dissatisfaction and hurt ego.

Sonya pretends that I'm not there, and just brushes past me without even the slightest glance in my direction. As she walks by, I steal a quick glance at the box. It seems that someone's been sacked. I wonder why Rocco would do it when she had nothing to do with what happened. It was all Hoffman.

I'm lost in thought, not even realizing that the elevator doors have closed, and it continues its route up and down the building. Not even slightly annoyed, I press the button for it to come again.

At that moment, I feel someone's hands around my waist, and I don't even need to turn around to know who it is. I smile, shaking my head.

"You know I don't like this lovey-dovey stuff at work," I pretend to frown.

"Why?" he whispers into my ear. "I own this building. Do you think anyone's gonna say anything?"

"No," I chuckle. "Of course not. I just don't want anyone to look at me differently just because I'm dating the big boss."

Dating the big boss.

Those words echo inside my mind, almost as loudly as church bells. I'm actually dating him. We've both said those dreaded words, and now, it seems like a huge burden has fallen off my back. I don't have to fight what I'm feeling anymore, I don't have to keep pushing him away.

I've realized that it doesn't matter how much time we have together, as long as it's time to remember. There are no guarantees in life. It could pass you by in a blink of an eye. You could die tomorrow and not do anything that's been on your to do list. But, what you can do is start living your life, day by day, expecting nothing but giving everything. And that's what I've decided to do with Rocco.

Strangely, it seems that he himself has reached the same conclusion, both of us walking on this life path together, hand in hand.

"I just want to make my own way," I explain.

He presses his lips to my neck.

"You are too sweet for your own good," he says. "Honestly, I doubted people like you even existed."

"Well, now you know we do," I smile at him, my hands covering his, the two of us still in a loving embrace, waiting for that elevator.

"I know, and I'm never letting you go...."

The elevator comes, and he places his hand before my eyes.

"I need you to trust me now," he tells me.

"What are you doing?" I feel a little nervous, but knowing he's here soothes me.

"Just let me guide you, OK?"

I'm listening to the sound of his voice and allowing his hands to push me forward. I feel the ground beneath my feet change in texture, and I know I'm inside the elevator. That knot tightens, reminding me that I'm still not rid of it. I probably never will be, even with Rocco by my side.

I hear the door close, then the barely tangible feeling of the elevator going up. I can feel Rocco's presence. His usual cologne is overpowering, tickling my brain, but at the same time providing a calming sensation.

"Do you trust me?" he asks.

"Of course," I say without any hesitation.

"Will you do what I ask of you?"

"Depends on what you're asking," I chuckle, his warm hand still over my eyes, the other around my waist. It feels safe to be hugged like this.

"I'm serious," he says softly, but gravely. "I will ask something of you now, something that might shock you. Will you do it?"

I realize that he is talking about something very important. I could tell from the sound of his voice, from the way his fingers were pressing into my waist, pulling me closer to him, so that now we looked like one body.

"I will," I nod.

I don't know what he wants, but there is no hesitation in my voice. There will never again be any hesitation with him. And I wanted him to be fully sure of that.

"Alright, Grace," he whispers from behind. "I am going to take my hand away from your eyes. And you are going to open them. Then, you will look down."

I gasp silently. Is he really asking me to do that? What if I vomit? What if I lose consciousness? What if... so many what ifs, one worse than the other.

Despite all those troublesome thoughts, I hear myself say yes.

"I will do it," I speak gently, but confidently.

I feel the pressure of his hand on my eyes diminish, until light from the elevator ceiling hits me, even through closed eyes. The other hand on my waist is still there, and I'm grateful for it.

I inhale deeply. Then, I open my eyes. I'm looking straight ahead at the buttons. I just need to do it quickly, like ripping off a band aid.

One.

Two.

Three.

I lower my head and look down.

There is no more glass floor. It has been changed, and all I see is a regular old grey floor. Nothing else. No wires, no weights pulling down as the elevator pulls up. No endless bottom. The knot in my stomach immediately loosens.

I turn to him quickly, my lips spread into a wide smile.

"What..." I ask, but I'm too shocked, too in awe to finish that thought.

"Is it better now?" he asks, his gaze a promise of eternal protection.

"You did this?" I gasp. "For me?"

He just nods instead of a reply. Looking at him, I finally see him for who he is, who he has always been. His hands will forever be my healing place. His words will always know how to sing the song my heart knows and recognizes. He will always be the light that guides me out of a dark tunnel and into the light.

Love. That is what he is.

I wrap my arms around his neck and kiss him. Our lips and tongues intertwine, until the ping of the elevator informs us that we've reached the desired floor. Hand in hand, we walk out, lingering in the still empty hallway of my floor.

"I don't know what to say," I manage to mutter.

I honestly don't know, because all I feel is this intense, but quiet emotion that has become an inextricable part of the very oxygen I breathe.

"Just say yes to everything I ask you," he smiles. "Like now."

His hand dives into his blazer pocket and he extracts a box. I stumble backwards in shock, and he grabs me by the hand, pulling me back to him.

"I always knew you'd fall for me hard," he chuckles.

"That is so corny," I laugh.

But it is who we are. This is the energy that has brought us together. A little bit contradictory, but more powerful than anything else I've ever felt before. There is a certain kind of freedom I've only come to know with him by my side, as we're both caught together in this divine spell.

He opens the box and shows me a ring. It's small. Dainty. The diamond is pear-shaped, sparkling in orange and yellow hues, like the summer rain. But its shine brightens a midsummer garden in full bloom bathed in the soft glow of the afternoon sun.

I give him my hand, and he puts the ring on my finger. I glance up, right into his eyes. I see myself in them. I see the feelings of my own heart mirrored in them.

"Yes," I say.

"Yes?" he asks.

"Yes!" I shout, wrapping my arms around his neck.

Feeling as if we are the only two people in all the world, I press my lips to his.

"I will always be whatever you need me to be, just as long as you are by my side," he tells me.

I know I've finally found what I didn't even know I was looking for. My hungry soul has found solace and nourishment in someone who understands me, who loves me, and I know now that whatever happens, he will always be the cradle for both my body and my heart.

*****

Don't miss out!

Visit the website below and you can sign up to receive emails whenever Erica Frost publishes a new book. There's no charge and no obligation.

https://books2read.com/r/B-A-YRSV-IXWDC

BOOKS 2 READ

Connecting independent readers to independent writers.

Also by Erica Frost

Seduced By A Billionaire
Dark Secrets
A Billionaire's Game
Power Play
Ruthless Rival
Taming The Billionaire
The Hated Billionaire
3-Pointer